The Banished
A Swabian Historical Tale
Vol. 3

By

Wilhelm Hauff

The Banished
A Swabian Historical Tale
Vol. 3
by Wilhelm Hauff

ISBN: 978-93-60466-42-8
Published by

DOUBLE 9 BOOKS

2/13-B, Ansari Road
Daryaganj, New Delhi – 110002
info@double9books.com
www.double9books.com
Tel. 011-40042856

ABOUT THE AUTHOR

The Württemberger artist and author Wilhelm Hauff was born on November 29, 1802, and died on November 18, 1827. Hauff was born in Stuttgart. His father, August Friedrich Hauff, was a secretary in the Württemberg ministry of foreign affairs, and his mother, Hedwig Wilhelmine Elsaesser Hauff, was a teacher. He was the second of four kids. When Hauff was seven years old, he lost his father. He learned most of what he knew in the library of his maternal grandfather in Tübingen, where his mother had moved after her husband died. From 1818 to 1820, he went to school at the University of Tübingen. In 1818, he was sent to the Klosterschule at Blaubeuren. He studied philosophy and theology at the Tübinger Stift for four years and was done. After graduating from college, Hauff worked as a tutor for the children of General Baron Ernst Eugen von Hugel (1774–1849), who was the minister of war for Württemberg. It was for these children that he wrote his Marchen (fairy tales), which were later collected in the Marchen Almanach auf das Jahr 1826 (Fairytale Almanac of 1826, also known as Tales of the Caravan, Inn, and Palace in the US).

CONTENTS

CHAPTER XXVI

The Duke at length is coming,
The battle field's not far;
For vanquish'd is the foeman,
And he brings the spoils of war.

G. Schwab.

A knight in armour, his horse being led between two of the lansquenet from the outpost, now approached the place where Long Peter, their general, and the other men, were assembled. Though he had drawn the vizor of his shining helmet over his face, the fifer of Hardt thought he recognised him as the man he expected, by the plates and cuish of steel which encased his muscular limbs, the plumes which waved high in the breeze, and the well known scarf which crossed over his coat of mail. And he was not mistaken, for one of the men who led his horse advanced to the General, and acquainted him that the noble "Knight of Sturmfeder" wished to speak to the leaders of the lansquenet.

Long Peter answered in the name of the rest, "tell him he is welcome, and that Peter Hunzinger the General, Staberl of Vienna, Conrad the Magdeburger, Balthaser Löffler, and the brave Muckerle, all well appointed Captains, are ready to receive and hear him. May my soul be punished, but he has a beautiful suit of armour, and an helmet fit for King Francis; and as to his steed, I have never seen a finer--*Morbleu*, how well he stands on his four legs!"

The men kept at a respectful distance from the stranger, who now approached, but shewed no inclination to dismount. Raising his vizor, he spoke to one of the men, and discovered his handsome friendly countenance. "Is not that Hans, the musician?" said he, to the men. "I have a word to say to him first."

The general made a sign to the fifer to approach the young knight, who immediately dismounted from his horse. "Welcome in Würtemberg, noble sir," said the man of Hardt, and returned a hearty shake of Albert von Sturmfeder's hand: "what news do you bring? The Duke's cause prospers, if I can judge from the expression of your countenance."

"Come on one side," he replied, in anxious haste. "How fares it in Lichtenstein? Have you a letter or a couple of lines for me? O give it quickly!"

The fifer smiled at the impatience of the lovesick youth; "I have neither letter nor line. The lady is well, and the old knight also; that is all I know."

"How!" replied the other, "nothing, not even a message? I am sure she did not let you depart without something for me!"

"When I took my leave of the lady the day before yesterday, she said, 'Tell him to hasten the entrance into Stuttgardt;' and when she spoke, became as red in the face as you are at present."

"We'll soon be there, with God's will!" he answered. "But how has she passed the long summer? I have only heard from her three times since we parted. Were you often in Lichtenstein, Hans?"

"Dear sir," answered the fifer, "have patience, and I will relate every thing, in length and breadth, on the march: for the present, be satisfied with the assurance, that so soon as the old knight hears you are advancing to Stuttgardt, he will set out from Lichtenstein with your bride, for he does not doubt of your overpowering the garrison. Have you succeeded in taking Heimsheim?"

"We have: I rode through the gates with twelve horsemen, before they were aware of our coming. Though the garrison were somewhat stronger than us, they were dispirited and dissatisfied. I treated with them in the Duke's name, and made them believe that he was coming up with a large body of troops, upon which they surrendered: thus far are we in Würtemberg. But in what state is the road before us?"

"Open, into the heart of the country, open. I have important news for the Duke from the knight of Lichtenstein, namely, that the men in power are out of the land, do you know----"

"Is it the meeting they now hold at Nördlingen you mean?" interrupted Albert. "Oh! yes, we know it, for it was that news which determined the Duke to commence operations."

"Well, when the cats are away, the mice will play," said the fifer; "the garrisons are every where careless. None of the League think any more of the Duke, their attention being wholly taken up with the meeting at Nördlingen, where it will be decided, whether Austria, or Bavaria, or Prince Christoph, or the Leaguist towns Augsburg and Aalen, Nürnberg, and Bopfinger, will reign over us."

"What long faces they will make," exclaimed Albert, smiling, "when they hear that the chair about which they are quarrelling is already possessed:

'The frog jumps into the muddy pool,

Tho' he may set upon a golden stool!'

says the proverb; they may shoulder their guns and give up governing now. And the Würtembergers, what are their feelings towards the Duke at present? Do you believe many will come to his assistance?"

"He may reckon upon the citizens and peasantry," replied the fifer. "How it stands with the knights, I don't know; for when I asked the old man of Lichtenstein, he shrugged up his shoulders and muttered a couple of curses: I fear that matter is not so well as it should be. But citizens and peasants hold to a man for their Prince. Many extraordinary signs have appeared, which encourage the people. Lately in the valley of the Rems a stone fell from the sky, on one side of which a stag's horn and the following words were engraved, 'Here's to good Würtemberg for ever,' and on the reverse, in Latin, 'Long live Duke Ulerich.'"

"Did you say it fell from the sky?"

"So it was said. The peasantry were overjoyed at it, but the officers of the League put the magistrate of the place where it had fallen into prison, and wanted to extort from him the name of the person who had engraved the letters. And when it was proclaimed, upon pain of severe punishment, that no one was to speak of the Duke, the men only laughed, and said, 'We dream of him now.' They all wish him back again, and would rather be oppressed by their legitimate Lord than be flayed by strangers."

"That's as it should be," said Albert. "The Duke and his cavalry may be here in a few hours. His intention is, to cut his way straight through the country to Stuttgardt. The capital once ours, the rest will soon follow. But how is it with these lansquenets--will they join us?"

"I had almost forgotten them," said Hans, "we had better go to them; else they will become impatient if we keep them waiting. You must be cautious how you treat them, for they are proud fellows, and have no small idea of their own importance. By winning these five to our interests, the whole twelve companies are sure to follow. With their General, Long Peter, mind and be very civil and courteous."

"Which is Long Peter?"

"The big man, sitting under the oak; he with the stiff mustachios and hat of distinction on his head. He is the commander in chief."

"I will talk to him, and follow your advice," Albert answered, and proceeded towards them. The long conversation which they had held had somewhat displeased the men, and little Muckerle in particular eyed the ambassador of the Duke with a penetrating glance. But when the young knight appeared among them his noble demeanour disconcerted them, they became shy and embarrassed before him, so much so, that the courteous words which he addressed to them soon had the desired effect of bringing them over to the Duke's cause. They listened to him in respectful silence.

"Most experienced general and brave commanders of the assembled lansquenet," said Albert, "the Duke of Würtemberg having approached the boundary of his country, and captured Heimsheim, is determined in the same way to recover his whole dukedom."

"May my soul be punished, but he is right!" said Long Peter; "I would do the same."

"He has already experienced the courage and military science of the lansquenet, when they fought on the side of his enemies, and he trusts they will manifest the same bravery in his cause, promising upon his princely word, faithfully to fulfil the engagements he has proposed."

"A pious man," murmured the commanders among themselves, with approving nods; "a gold florin a month, and, *morbleu*! four measures of wine a day for the superior officers."

The general rose from his seat, saluted him by uncovering his bald head, and said, though often interrupted by many coughs of embarrassment, "We thank you, most noble sir; we agree--we'll join you. We'll give back to the Swabian League what they gave us, that we will--hard usage. The very best and most courageous, as well as the most excellent of men, have they dismissed, as if they did not value our services. There stands, for example, Captain Löffler: if there is a braver lansquenet in all Christendom, I'll allow my skin to be peeled off and walk about in my bones the rest of my life! Look at Staberl of Vienna: the sun and moon have never shone upon his equal! And the Magdeburger there, no Turk ever fought like him; and as for little Muckerle, though he does not look it, he is the best shot in the world, and can hit the bull's eye in the target at forty paces. I won't say anything of myself; self praise does not sound well. But, *bassa manelka*! I have served in Spain and Holland--and, *canto cacramento*--also in Italy and Germany! *Morbleu!* Long Peter is known in every army. May my soul be punished, when I and the others get behind the Swabian dogs, *diavolo maledetto*, they'll take to their hareskin, and be off as fast as their heels can carry them!"

This was the longest speech Long Peter had ever made; and when many years after he sealed the renown of the German lansquenet with his death before Pavia, his companions, in relating to their young comrades the events of his life, always mentioned this moment as the most glorious of his career. He was described as standing before his audience, leaning upon his long sword, his large hat with the red feathers cocked over his ear, the right hand resting upon his side, and his legs spread out, wanting nothing to complete his pretensions to a regular general than a better jerkin and the chain of honour.

The commanders, after the flattering speech of their general, invited their new guest to pass their army in review. The hollow sound of enormous drums soon roused the men from their rest. They appeared still to be under the influence of Fronsberg's military genius and strict discipline, by the activity they displayed in forming themselves, in a few moments, into three great circles, each composed of four companies. To an eye accustomed, as in our times, to the rapid but steady movements of regiments, and the beautiful appearance of their uniformity of dress, the sight of this heterogeneous multitude would cause surprise if not ridicule. Though the lansquenets were generally clothed according to their own taste, there was still a semblance of an attempt to uniformity after the fashion of those days. For the most part they wore jerkins of leather setting tight to the body, or leather waistcoats with arms of coarse cloth, and enormous wide trousers tied under the knee, and falling by their own weight a little below it. The legs were covered with coarse stockings of a light colour, and the feet with shoes of untanned leather. A hat, leather or metal cap, probably articles of plunder rather than of purchase, covered the head; and the bearded faces of these men, many of whom had served twenty years in all the armies and under every climate in Europe, gave them a very bold and martial appearance. They were armed with a dagger and halberd, and some with guns, which were fired with a match.

Standing with outstretched legs, and foot to foot meeting, they presented a bold front; and Albert's military spirit rejoiced at the sight of these experienced warriors, who, however, were well aware, that in single combat they had no confidence, but formed in mass they were formidable even to a more numerous enemy.

The commanders had carefully retained all the manœuvres and words of command of their former leader. They walked into the middle of one of the circles, followed by their new acquaintance, when the deep and loud-toned voice of Long Peter gave the word "Attention! face about."

The celerity with which the order was obeyed by turning around facing inwards, proved they had not forgotten their lesson. They listened to the proposals of the Duke of Würtemberg which the commanders addressed to them, and manifested by a murmur which ran through the ranks, that they were satisfied with the terms, and would serve his cause with the same zeal as they had not long since served against it. They were then put through several manœuvres, which they performed with an address that astonished Albert, who thought the art of war of his day would never be surpassed as long as the world existed. But he deceived himself. His error of judgment was, however, pardonable, for in the same way did our grandfathers hold the heroes of Frederick the Great in estimation, as the *ne plus ultra* of military discipline, and did not anticipate the ridicule of their descendants on the subject of perruques and long gaiters. And may not the time come, when the *good old times* of 1839 will also have their share of ridicule? Certainly such elegant laced-up figures as are seen now-a-days among military men, were not the fashion among the lansquenet and their commanders, A. D. 1519.

About an hour after, it was announced from the advanced posts, that they had perceived at the further end of the valley, in the neighbourhood of the road leading from Heimsheim, the glittering of arms, and when they put their ears close to the ground, they heard distinctly the trampling of many horses.

"That's the Duke," cried Albert; "bring me my horse; I will ride and meet him."

The young man galloped away through the wood, to the admiration of the bystanders, who were astonished at the activity he displayed in throwing himself upon his steed, encumbered as he was with his heavy armour. Helmets with high plumes and shining lances were shortly after seen moving among the bushes of the valley. As they approached, the cavalry issued from the wood, seen first breast high among the underwood, and then their whole figures were visible on a small height, where the whole body assembled. The joy of the fifer of Hardt was indescribable when he got a sight of the gallant band, headed by the Duke. He took the general by the hand, and pointed to them with an air of triumphant satisfaction.

"Which is the Duke?" asked Long Peter; "is that him on the black piebald horse?"

"No, that is the noble knight Von Hewen: the banner-bearer of Würtemberg:--but, no, am I mistaken? I declare Albert von Sturmfeder carries it!"

"That's a great honour! *Morbleu*, he is only five-and-twenty, and carries the flag! In France the only man who is entitled to that privilege is the constable, the next man to the king in honour. In that country it is called the standard, and is made all of gold. But which is Duke Ulerich?"

"Do you see that man in a green cloak, with the black and red feathers in his helmet? he that rides next to the banner, mounted on a black horse, and is speaking to the young knight. He points this way. That's the Duke."

The body of cavalry was composed of about forty men, mostly noblemen and their servants, who the Duke, in his banishment, had assembled together, or appointed to meet him on the boundary of his country, when his plans were ripe for an invasion. They were all well mounted and armed. Albert von Sturmfeder carried Würtemberg's banner; next to him rode the Duke in complete armour. When they came within about two hundred paces of the lansquenet, Long Peter, in a loud voice, said to his people, "Attention, my people. When his Grace is near enough, and I raise my hat off my head, let every one cry, 'Vivat Ulericus!' lower the colours, and you, drummers, rattle upon your sheep-skins like thunder and lightning! Give us the animating flourish of the drum as at the storming of a fortress! *Bassa manelka*, beat away till the drumsticks break--that's the way the brave lansquenet salute a prince."

This short speech had the desired effect. The Duke's praises were murmured through the warlike band; they shook their halberds, stamped their fire-arms clattering on the ground, the drummers prepared their drums and sticks to obey their general's orders in full vigour; and when Albert von Sturmfeder, the standard-bearer of Würtemberg, sprang forward, followed by Duke Ulerich, majestic as in the best days of his power, with bold dignified countenance, Long Peter uncovered his head in respectful submission, the preconcerted signal was instantly obeyed, the drummers executed their military music, the colours were lowered in salute, and the whole body of the lansquenet vociferated a loud and cheering "Vivat Ulericus!"

The peasant of Hardt remained at a distance, not heeding the salute, for his whole soul appeared concentred in his eye, which was fixed on his lord in the intoxication of joy. The Duke stopped his horse, and looked about him in the dead silence which afterwards succeeded. The fifer then came forward, knelt down, holding his stirrup for him to dismount, and said, "Here's to good Würtemberg for ever!"

"Ha! are you there, Hans, my trusty companion in misfortune, the first to salute me in Würtemberg? I expected my nobles would have been the foremost to greet my arrival in my country, my chancellor and my council--where are the dogs? Where are the representatives of my estates? will they not welcome me to my home? Is no one here to hold my stirrup but this peasant?"

The followers of the Duke hastened around him in surprise when they heard these cutting words. They scarcely knew whether he was in earnest, or whether it was a mere sarcastic joke over his own misfortunes. His mouth, appeared to smile, but his eye bespoke anger, and his voice sounded stern and commanding. They looked at each other in doubtful apprehension as to the meaning of this burst of passion, when the fifer of Hardt replied,

"For this once a peasant only assists your Grace on Würtemberg ground; but despise not a true heart and a willing hand. The others will soon come, when they hear the Duke treads his native land again."

"Do you think so?" said Ulerich, with a bitter smile, as he swung himself from his horse; "do you think they'll come? Hitherto we have little reason to flatter ourselves; but I'll knock at their doors, and let them know that the old gentleman is there, and will have admittance to his house! Are these the lansquenets who have agreed to serve me?" he continued, attentively observing the little army; "they appear well armed, and in good condition. How many men are there?"

"Twelve companies, your Grace," answered Peter the general, who still stood without his hat, in a state of embarrassment, twisting his mustachios occasionally. "Nothing but well-trained men. May my soul be punished--pardon my oath--but the king of France has no better soldiers!"

"Who are you?" asked the Duke, looking with astonishment at the large heavy figure of the general, with his immense sword and red face.

"I am a lansquenet of my own order, and am called Long Peter, but now the well-appointed general of the assembled----"

"What, general! this folly must have an end. You may be a very brave man, but you are not made to command. I will be your general henceforth," said the Duke, "and my knights will be named as your captains."

"*Bassa manelka!*--I am sorry I swore, but permit an old soldier to say a word to your Grace. What you propose would be against our terms of a gold florin a month, and four measures of wine a-day. There stands, for example, Staberl of Vienna, not a braver man under the sun----"

"Very good, very good, old man! we'll not talk of the gold florin and wine now," replied the Duke. "The captains shall retain their present commands, but I command you. Have you any ammunition?"

"Yes, to be sure," said the Magdeburger; "we have plenty, which belonged to your Grace, and which we brought away from Tübingen. Each man has eighty rounds."

"Very well," answered the Duke; "George von Hewen and Philip von Rechberg, do you divide the men, and each take six companies. Let their captains remain with their men, and assist their commanders. Ludwig von Gemmingen, I appoint you to command all the infantry. And now we'll march direct for Leonberg. Rejoice, my faithful standard bearer," said the Duke, as he mounted, "with God's assistance we'll be in Stuttgardt tomorrow."

The troop of cavalry, with the Duke at their head, led the way. Long Peter stood fixed in the same place, with his hat and its cock's feathers in his hand, observing the horsemen.

"That is a Prince, indeed!" he said to the other commanders who stood beside him. "What a powerful voice he has; and when he rolls his eyes about it makes one quake for fear! I thought he would have swallowed me, head and all, when he asked me who I was."

"I felt much in the same state as if hot water had been poured over me," said the Magdeburger. "This man is more to be dreaded than the Emperor in Vienna."

"Our reign has been but a short one," said Captain Muckerle; "our dignity has not lasted long."

"Fool! so much the better. Dignity only brings cares, says the proverb; our people don't submit readily to our orders--*diavolo!*--for one of them laughed at me in my face only this day. Things will go much better when the knights lead us: and we shall receive a gold florin and four measures of wine; that's our principal business." So said Peter.

"I think so too," said the Magdeburger; "and we have to thank Long Peter for our good fortune. Long may he live!"

"Thank you," said the general; "but I tell you, the Duke will set the League in flames again, *morbleu!* and when he draws his sword, he alone will hunt them out of the country. And did you hear how he cursed his council, chancellor, and nobles? I would not like to be in their skins."

The conversation of the veterans was now interrupted by the rolling of the drums, which no longer sounded at their command. Long Peter had been so often accustomed, during his many campaigns, to the vicissitudes of fortune, by being raised and lowered suddenly in rank, that he was not disconcerted by his present loss of command. He very quietly deprived his large hat of its ornamental cock's feather; he laid aside his red scarf and long sword, the emblems of his dignity, and shouldered his halberd. "May my soul be punished, but mine is a hard case, who but yesterday was in supreme command, and am now obliged to go back into the ranks," said he, as he took his place among his comrades. "But by Saint Peter, my holy patron and brother lansquenet, every thing is for the best in this world." His companions shook him by the hand, and agreed with him in his sentiments. It did his brave heart good to hear them approve of his conduct, the short time he had wielded the command over them. The three knights, their newly appointed leaders, mounted and put themselves at the head of their brigades; the lansquenets arranged themselves in the common order of march, and, Ludwig von Gemmingen ordering the drums to beat the advance, the little army broke up their camp, and set forward.

CHAPTER XXVII

The summit of the wall is gain'd
All in the silent night,
And now the fortress is attain'd!
We do not fear the light.
Now, let us sound the battle cry,
And be it "Death or victory!"

Schiller.

Duke Ulerich appeared before the gate of Stuttgardt, called the Red Hill Gate, on the night previous to the holiday of the Assumption of the Virgin Mary. Having captured the little town of Leonberg on his way, he prosecuted his march on the capital without further interruption. The news of his being in the country spread through the land like wild-fire, and judging by the numbers that joined his colours, as well as by the joy with which he was everywhere received, he had reason to suppose the people would rejoice to see their legitimate Prince re-established in his rights, and the hateful government of the League abolished.

The intelligence of his advance had reached Stuttgardt, and had caused much difference of feeling amongst its inhabitants. The nobility scarcely knew what they had to expect from the Duke; the shameful surrender of Tübingen being an event of too recent a date to leave them wholly without fear of his wrath. But the recollection of the brilliant court of Ulerich von Würtemberg and the merry days they had formerly passed under his sway, compared to the oppressions the League had inflicted on them, led them to incline to submission. Not a few, however, among them had reason to dread his return. The citizens could scarcely restrain their joy; and, quitting their houses, assembled in groups about the streets, talking over coming events. They cursed the League in strong terms, but silently, clenching their fists in their pockets, and were beyond measure patriotically inclined, and full of pugnacious propensities. Calling to mind the illustrious ancestors of their exiled Prince, whose name of Würtemberg they themselves bore; they reckoned up the many noble lords sprung from the same family, under whom they and their fathers had lived happily, and whose glorious deeds had spread their country's fame abroad. But the most important topic of their conversation was, that upon them depended, in a great measure, the decision of the struggle between the League and the Duke, as the whole country would now look upon the Stuttgardters as the fuglemen in the contest. They were, however, no way inclined of themselves to create an insurrection against the garrison of the League, whom they still feared, but they whispered to each other: "Brother, wait a little, and we'll soon have an opportunity to show those Leaguists what we Stuttgardters are made of."

The insurrectionary spirit of the burghers did not escape the notice of Christoph Schwarzenberg, the Leaguist governor. He perceived, but too late, the mistake that had been committed in disbanding the army. He applied to the representatives of his party assembled at Nördlingen for assistance, but gave them no hope of holding Stuttgardt unless they sent immediate relief. Scarcely had he time to make some feeble preparations for defence, when the rapid advance of the Duke checked his ardour. Perceiving he could not trust the citizens, that the nobles would not stand by him, and aware that the garrison was not strong enough even to ensure the safety of the gates of the city, he absconded in the night with the state council to Esslingen. Their flight was so sudden and secret, that their families even were ignorant of it, and no one in the town suspected the intentions of the governor and his senate. The partisans of the League, therefore, never dreaming of the desertion of their chiefs, treated the news of the approach of the Duke with indifference, for they did not believe the report of his being in the immediate neighbourhood.

The market-place in those days stood in the heart of the city. But even then two considerable suburbs, the Saint Leonhard and the field of tournament, were built around the town, provided with outer ditches, walls, and strong gates, which gave them also the appearance of fortified cities. They were separated from the old town which possessed its own walls and gates, and its inhabitants looked down with contempt on those of the suburbs. The market-place was the spot where the burghers were accustomed to assemble, according to the fashion of olden times when any extraordinary occurrence took place; and therefore, on the eventful evening before the day of the Assumption of the Virgin, the citizens streamed in crowds to this central point. Though every man in those days carried arms with impunity, which gave to an assembled multitude a fearful appearance, still the honest burghers of Stuttgardt would not have dared to utter, in the day-time, what they now ventured to do in the dusk. Had many of them been asked their opinion of the Duke in the forenoon, they would have answered, "What do I care about him? I am a peaceable citizen:" but upon this occasion, they raised their voices, I and cried, "We'll open the gates to the Duke! away with the Leaguists! Würtemberg for ever!"

The moon shone bright on the assembled crowd, which waved to and fro in restless motion, whilst a confused murmur seemed to indicate indecision as to what was to be done, perhaps because no one was bold enough to put himself forward on the occasion. Many heads looked out of the windows of the gable-ended houses which surrounded the market-place; they were the wives and families of the congregated citizens, listening with intense anxiety to what was going on: for it must be observed that the Stuttgardt ladies were in those days equally given to curiosity as they now are, and in their hearts pitied the Duke.

The hum of voices became louder and louder, whilst the feeling which ran through the crowd became more distinct. The cry "let's drive; the soldiers from the gates, and open them to the Duke," passed from mouth to mouth, when a tall, meagre-looking man was seen to spring up on a stone bank which surrounded the fountain, whence he overlooked the assemblage of burghers. He flourished his long arms about in the air, opened his large mouth, and hallooed with all his might to obtain a hearing. The noise about him having partially subsided, a few detached words and sentences were heard by the immediate bystanders. "What! do the honourable burghers of Stuttgardt intend to break the oath which they have sworn to the League? To whom do you want to open the gates--to the Duke? He can't have a very strong force with him, for he has no money to pay them, and he will make you open your purses. If you surrender to him, you will have ten thousand florins to pay. Do you hear? ten thousand florins, I say!"

"Who is that lanky fellow?" the citizens asked one another. "He's right," said one of them, "we shall have to pay handsomely."--"Is he a citizen, that man up there?"--"Who are you?" said one of the boldest; "how do you know we shall have to pay?"

"I am the renowned Doctor Calmus," said the speaker, with solemn voice, "and am quite sure of it. And who do you want to drive away? The Emperor, the Empire, the League? Will you run your heads against so many rich lords? and why? for Duke Utz, who only throws dust in your eyes! Do you forget his oppressive game laws, the least part of his tyranny? He has no more money left; he is a beggar, and has squandered everything in Mömpelgard----"

"Make him keep silence!" cried the burghers: "What is that to you? you are not one of our citizens; away with the bald-headed mouse,--kill him,-- throw him into the fountain to feed the fish!--Long live the Duke!"

Doctor Calmus raised his voice again, but was overpowered by the loud shouts of the bystanders.

At this moment another troop of burghers arrived in great haste from the suburbs. "The Duke is before the Red Hill gate," they cried, "with cavalry and infantry. Where is the governor and his council? He will fire into the town if the gates be not instantly opened! Away with the Leaguists!--Who is a good Würtemberger?"

The tumult increased. Perceiving the crowd still undecided, another speaker mounted the bank: he was a comely-looking man, who, for a moment, imposed on the crowd by his outward appearance. "Consider, honourable men," he cried: "what will the illustrious council of the League say if you----"

"Out with the illustrious council!" they answered, "away with him, tear him down, him with the rose-coloured cloak and smooth hair, he is an Ulmer--at him, he is an Ulmer!"

But before they could put their threats into execution, a powerful man stept up between the two orators, knocked the Doctor over with his right hand, and the Ulmer with his left, waving his cap in the air to obtain a hearing. "Silence! that is Hartman," whispered the burghers, "he understands the world; listen to what he says!"

"Hear me!" said he: "the governor and his council are nowhere to be found, they have fled, and left us in the lurch; we'll therefore seize these two, and keep them as hostages. And now to the Red Hill gate; our true Duke stands before it: it is better to open the gate of our own accord than that he should use force to do so. Who's a good Würtemberger, let him follow me."

He descended from his position, and was joyfully received by the crowd. The two advocates of the League were bound and led away before they had time to look about them. The stream of burghers now flowed from the marketplace through the upper gate and over the broad ditch of the old town leading to the field of tournament, and, passing the fortification, arrived at the Red Hill gate. The Leaguist troops, who occupied it, were soon overpowered, the gate was opened, the drawbridge fell, and laid over the town ditch.

The leader of the Duke's infantry had, during these occurrences in the town, stationed his best troops at this gate, as it was doubtful what steps the League would take at the approach of the Duke. Ulerich himself had examined the post. In vain did Albert von Sturmfeder endeavour to persuade him that the garrison of Stuttgardt was too weak to make any formidable resistance, in vain did he represent to him the desire the burghers had to see him again, and would willingly open the gates, the Duke looked darker than the night, pressed his lips together, and gnashed his teeth in anger.

"You don't understand these things," he muttered to the young man; "you don't know the world; they are all false; never trust any one but yourself. They accommodate themselves to every change of wind. But I have them this once under my thumb. Do you suppose I have been obliged to turn my back upon my country to no purpose?"

Albert was unable to comprehend the Duke's meaning. He had seen him firm in misfortune, yea even mild and gentle, and in speaking of the many beneficent plans for the good of his people, which he intended to put into execution when he returned to his country, he had seldom manifested any violent fits of passion in talking of his enemies, and scarcely ever betrayed any ill will towards his subjects, who had deserted him. But whether it was the sight of his country that awakened the feeling of vexation stronger in him than usual, whether he was irritated that the nobility and representatives of his estates had not come forward to welcome his arrival after he had passed the boundary of Würtemberg; whatever was the cause, his spirits were no longer cheerful and buoyant. His look appeared as if troubled by a thirst for revenge, and a certain severity and harshness in giving his opinion, struck those about him as indications of alteration in his temper. Albert von Sturmfeder, in particular, could not account for this new turn in Ulerich's manner.

The town had been summoned more than half an hour. The time which had been given was nearly expired, and still no answer had arrived. The hum of voices was heard in the town, and a restless moving about the streets, shewing that the besieged were doubtful whether their terms would be accepted or not.

The Duke rode up to the lansquenets, who were resting on their halberds and match guns, headed by their leaders, who were each occupied in preserving discipline among their men. Albert remarked the countenance of the Duke by the light of the moon. The veins of his of his forehead were swollen beyond their common size, his cheeks being deeply flushed, and his eyes sparkled like fire.

"Hewen! get the scaling ladders ready," said the Duke with a stern voice. "Thunder and lightning! I stand before my own house, and they will not let me in. The trumpets shall sound once more, when, if they don't open the gates instantly, I'll fire the town and burn it to the ground."

"*Bassa manelka!* that's what I like," said Long Peter to his comrade, who stood in the front rank near the Duke. "The ladders are going to be brought, we'll climb up like cats, and drive those fellows from the walls, and then the musqueteers will pepper them properly, *canto cacramento!*"

"Ah! yes," said the Magdeburger, "and then we'll sally into the town, set fire to all corners--plunder--burst open the doors--that's the fun for us lansquenets!"

"For God's sake, my Lord Duke," said Albert, who had heard his last words, and had observed the rapacious spirit which animated the soldiers, "only wait a short quarter of an hour longer; recollect it is your own capital. They are most likely still deliberating."

"What have they got to consult so long about?" replied Ulerich with ill humour: "their rightful lord stands before his own gate, and demands admittance. My patience is already exhausted. Spread my banner to the light of the moon, Albert; let the trumpets sound; summon the town once more for the last time; and if the gates are not opened by the time I have counted thirty after the last word, by the holy Hubertus, I'll storm the walls. Be quick! Albert."

"O sir! consider your town, your best town! Having lived so long in it, would you now give it to the flames? Give them a little more time."

"Ha!" laughed the Duke in anger, and struck the armour of his breast with his steel glove, which sounded through the stillness of the night, "I see you are not inclined to enter Stuttgardt, and merit your wife thereby. But no more words now, at the risk of my displeasure, Albert von Sturmfeder. Obey my order quickly: unfurl my banner, let the trumpet sound! sound and frighten the dogs out of their sleep, that they may know a Würtemberger stands here, and will enter his house in spite of the Emperor and Empire. I say, summon them again, Sturmfeder!"

The young man obeyed the order in silence, and riding close up to the ditch, unfurled Würtemberg's banner. The rays of the moon appeared to welcome it back to its country, and shone full upon it, whereby the four fields with their charges were plainly exhibited to view. On a large flag of red silk were wove the arms of Würtemberg, with its escutcheon and four fields. In the first were the stag horns of Würtemberg, in the second the balls of Teck, the third had the storming flag of the empire, which belonged by right to the Duke as banner-bearer of the empire, and in the fourth were the fish of Mömpelgard: the whole being surmounted by the crown and the bugle of Urach. The strong arm of the young man could scarcely hold the heavy flag in the breeze. He was attended by three trumpeters, who now sounded their wild tones before the closed gate.

A window above it opened, and a voice asked their business. Albert von Sturmfeder answered, "Ulerich, by the grace of God Duke of Würtemberg and Teck, Count of Urach and Mömpelgard, summons for the second and last time his city of Stuttgardt, to open its gates willingly and instantly to him, else he will storm the walls and treat the town as an enemy."

During the time Albert was delivering his message, a confused noise as of a crowd in motion mingled with voices in the streets was heard, which approaching nearer and nearer, at length broke out into tumult and shouting.

"May my soul be punished, if they are not about to make a sortie!" said Long Peter, loud enough to be heard by the Duke.

"Perhaps you are right," answered the Duke, turning abruptly to the startled lansquenet: "close in together, present your pikes, and have the matches ready, that we may receive them as they deserve."

The whole line retreated some distance from the ditch, leaving only the three first companies at the point where the drawbridge fell. A wall of pikes bristled in formidable array against a sudden attack, the guns were presented and the match held at the touchhole ready to fire. The dead stillness of expectation which reigned without the walls was broken by the tumultuous noise within the town. The drawbridge fell, but no enemy sallied forth to repel the invaders: three old grey-headed men alone proceeded through the gate, bearing the arms of the city, with its keys.

When the Duke saw the peaceable mission approach, he rode towards them in a friendly manner, followed by Albert. Two of these men appeared to be councillors or magistrates: they bent their knee before their lord and master, and tendered him the proofs of their submission. He gave them to his attendants, and said to the ambassadors, "You have kept us waiting somewhat long outside: truly we should very shortly have mounted the walls, and have lighted up your town with our own hands, and made your eyes smart with the smoke of it. Why did you keep us waiting so long?"

"Oh, my Lord!" said one of the old men, "as far as the burghers were concerned they were ready to open the gates instantly; but we have some few principal members of the League still among us, who held long and dangerous speeches to the people to instigate them to rebellion against your grace. That is the true cause of the delay."

"Ha! who are those men?" said the Duke. "I hope you have taken care not to let them escape, for I would like to say a word to them."

"God forbid, your highness! we know our duty to our lord, and therefore seized them immediately and put them in confinement. Is it your wish to see them?"

"To-morrow morning in the castle, I'll examine them. Send to the executioner at the same time; perhaps it will be requisite to take their heads off."

"Prompt justice, just what they deserve," said a shrill croaking voice behind the two burghers.

"Who is it that interrupts me?" said the Duke, when looking around, an extraordinary figure of diminutive size stepped forward, carrying a hump with which nature had ornamented his back, and which was concealed under a black silk cloak. His well-combed grey locks were covered by a small pointed hat; a pair of eyes, which bespoke cunning and intrigue, sparkled under bushy grey eyebrows; and a thin moustache, which sprung out from under an eagle-like nose, gave him much the appearance of a feline animal. An expression of fawning courteousness lay upon his wrinkled features, and when he uncovered his head at the Duke's salute, Albert felt an insuperable disgust and a peculiar abhorrence at the sight of him.

The Duke, when he noticed the little man, called to him in a friendly way: "Ha! Ambrosius Bolland, our chancellor! are you still alive? You might have made your appearance before now, methinks, for you must have known we were in our country again; but you are, notwithstanding, welcome to us."

"Most illustrious Duke!" answered the chancellor, Ambrosius Bolland, "I have been laid up with a violent fit of gout, which would scarcely allow me to leave my house; pardon me, therefore, your----"

"Very well, very well," said the Duke, smiling, "I'll soon cure you of the gout. Come to us in the castle to-morrow morning; it is our pleasure at present to ride through the town. Forwards, my faithful banner-bearer!" he turned to Albert, with gracious demeanour, "you have kept your word honestly as far as the gates of Stuttgardt; I will reward your faithful service. By Saint Hubertus, the bride is yours according to justice and right. Carry my flag before me, we'll plant it on my castle, and tread the Leaguist banner in the dust! Gemmingen and Hewen, you are my guests for the night; we'll see if the lords of the Swabian League have left us any of our old wine."

Thus rode Duke Ulerich, surrounded by his knights, who had followed him in his train through the gates of his capital. The burghers received him with loud *vivas*, and the pretty damsels in the windows waved their white handkerchiefs, to the annoyance of their mothers, who thought these salutations were directed to the handsome young knight carrying the Duke's banner, and who, as seen by the light of their torches, recalled to their minds St. George, the dragon-killer.

CHAPTER XXVIII

Oh, may the deeds of those no more,

The glory that they won,

The sire's spirit hovering o'er,

So stimulate the son,

That this day's setting sun may see

Of no degenerate clay are we.

P. Conz.

When Albert von Sturmfeder viewed the old castle of Stuttgardt the next morning, it did not exhibit the same form which it has in our days, the present one having been built by the Duke's son, Prince Christoph. The residence of the former Dukes of Würtemberg stood in the same place; and differed little in plan and appearance from Christoph's work, except that it was for the most part built of wood. Being surrounded by broad and deep ditches, over which a bridge led to the town, a large open space in front served in early times as a tilt-yard for the gay court of Ulerich, whose powerful hand had often rolled many a knight in the arena. The interior also of the building bespoke the customs and usages of the times. High and vaulted halls occupied the lower part of the castle, and were generally used in rainy weather as a place for manly exercises, having space sufficient to admit of the largest lance being wielded without hindrance. Old chronicles mention the size of these halls as being spacious enough to contain between two and three hundred persons at table. A broad stone staircase, capable of admitting two horsemen to ride abreast, and made for that purpose, led to the upper apartments, where the splendour of the rooms, the grandeur of the hall of the knights, and the richly ornamented galleries used for dancing and play, corresponded with the exterior appearance of the castle.

Albert viewed with an eye of astonishment the extravagant splendour of the palace. When he compared the establishment of his ancestors with what he now saw, how small and confined they seemed to him! He recollected the stories he had heard of the brilliancy of Ulerich's court, on the occasion of his magnificent marriage, when seven thousand guests, from all parts of the German empire, caroused in this castle, in whose vaulted halls and spacious court-yards all kinds of games and merrymaking were held for a whole month; and a numerous assembly of noblemen, with all the greatest beauties of the day, kept up the merry dance till late at night. He looked down into the garden of the castle, which, from its beauty, was called Paradise. His fancy peopled the shaded walks and summerhouses, which were scattered about it, with the joyous throng of gallant knights and stately ladies, enjoying themselves with mirth and song. But alas! how deserted and empty were they now; and when he compared their present state with the picture his imagination had created, what a lesson of this world's vanity did it not give! The guests of the marriage feast, the brilliant merry court, all are vanished, said he to himself; the princely bride is flown, the brilliant circle of women by whom she was surrounded scattered to the four winds; knights and counts, who once feasted in these halls, have deserted their prince; the tender pledges of his marriage now in a distant land, in the hands of his enemies; and the lord of the castle is left alone to brood in solitude over his misfortunes, and think only of revenge; and who knows how long he will be allowed to remain in the house of his ancestors; who knows whether his enemies will not get the upper hand again, and, overpowering him, drive him into misery twofold greater than what he has already experienced.

The young soldier attempted in vain to repress these gloomy thoughts, which the contrast between the splendour of the surrounding objects and the misfortunes of the Duke involuntarily awakened in his mind. In vain he summoned to his aid the portrait of that beloved being, whom he hoped soon to call his own for ever; in vain he painted, in the most glowing colours, to his imagination, all the charms of domestic happiness in her company; he was still unable to shake off the gloomy ideas which the sight of the castle had produced on his mind. Whatever was the cause of it, whether it was the Duke's lofty character, which he had so nobly manifested in misfortune, and which had created so deep a feeling of admiration in the breast of the young man, or whether nature had gifted him with an extraordinary perception into future events, he remained riveted to the spot in deep thought. Persuaded that the Duke's affairs were any thing but prosperous, he felt himself in duty bound to warn him against some unforeseen impending danger which irresistibly haunted his mind.

"Why so much wrapped in thought, young man?" asked an unknown voice behind him, and roused him from his reverie: "I should have thought Albert von Sturmfeder had reason to be of good cheer."

Albert turned round in surprise, and cast his eyes upon the chancellor, Ambrosius Holland. If this man had struck Albert the night before, as being peculiarly forbidding by his officious courteousness, his cat-like sneaking manner, he was now more confirmed in his dislike, when he remarked the deformity of his person, rendered more conspicuous by an overladen finery of dress. His dark-yellow shrivelled-up face, with an eternal hypocritical smile upon it, his green eyes peeping out under long grey eyelashes, his highly inflamed eyelids, and scanty beard, contrasted strangely with a red velvet cap, and a gown made of bright yellow silk, which hung over his hump. Under the gown he wore a grass-green dress, slashed with rose-coloured silk, his knee-bands being of the same material, fastened with enormous rosettes. His head was stuck close between his shoulders, and the red cap, which he carried on it, appeared to belong equally to the hump. It was a great joke of the executioner of Stuttgardt, that of all heads, that of the chancellor Ambrosius Bolland would appear to be the most difficult to cut off.

This was the man who looked up at Albert von Sturmfeder with a courteous smile. He addressed him with smooth words, "Perhaps you don't know me, my much esteemed young friend: I am Ambrosius Bolland, the chancellor of his highness. I come to wish you a good morning."

"I thank you," said Albert; "and esteem it a great honour, if you have put yourself out of your way on my account."

"Honour to whom honour is due! you are the pattern and crown of our young knighthood! Truly, you who have stood by my master so faithfully in his necessity and dangers have a claim to my most inward thanks, and my particular respect."

"You might have bought your compliments much cheaper had you joined us at Mömpelgard," replied Albert, who was offended by the adulation of the flatterer. "There is no necessity to speak of fidelity; it were better to reprove the want of it."

A momentary ray of anger shot from the green-eyed chancellor, but he soon regained his fawning manner. "To be sure, I am of the same opinion. For my part, I was so crippled with gout, I could not travel to Mömpelgard; but now, what little power heaven has left me shall be devoted with redoubled zeal to the Duke's service."

He paused a moment, expecting an answer; but Albert was silent, and eyed him with a glance which he did not well know how to interpret. "Well, but you will now be able to enjoy your prosperity," continued the chancellor; "of course it is nothing more than you deserve, and the Duke has well chosen his favourite. Will you allow Ambrosius Bolland also to acknowledge his sense of your services? Are you an amateur of curious arms? Come to my dwelling in the market-place, and choose what most pleases you out of my armoury. If you are a lover of rare books, I have a whole chest full, much at your disposal, and pray select any you may fancy, as is the custom among friends. Come and dine with me sometimes; my niece keeps house for me, a pretty girl of seventeen years; only I must beg of you--hi! hi! hi!--not to look at her too close."

"Don't be afraid; I am already engaged."

"So? ah, that's acting like a Christian; it's very praiseworthy. It is not always that we find such virtue among the youth of the present day. I was quite certain that Sturmfeder was a pattern of virtue. But what I wanted to say was, that we--being the only two as yet who compose the Duke's court--we must keep together, and not allow any one to be appointed without our consent. Do you understand me? hi! hi!--one hand washes the other. But we can talk over that some other time. You will honour me with a visit sometimes?"

"When my time will allow me, Chancellor Ambrosius Bolland."

"I would willingly remain longer in your society, for your presence does my heart good; but I must now to the Duke. He is going to sit in judgment this morning on two prisoners who tried to excite the people to rebellion against him last night. Who would bet that Beltler was not already appointed."

"Beltler!" asked Albert, "who is he?"

"He is the executioner, most worthy young friend."

"For heaven's sake! the Duke surely will not stain the first day of his new government with blood!"

The chancellor smiled bitterly, and answered: "You do honour again to your excellent heart, but you are not fit to sit in a court of criminal justice. Examples must be made. One of them," he continued, with a soft voice, "will be beheaded because he belongs to the nobility, and the other, being a low fellow, will be hanged. God bless you, my dear friend!"

With these words the chancellor departed, treading with light step the long gallery which led to the Duke's apartment. Albert followed him with a look of contempt and disdain. He had heard that this man formerly, either by prudence, or, perhaps, rather by an unwarrantable exercise of artful cunning, had gained great influence over Ulerich: he had often heard the Duke himself speak of the great confidence he had in his cleverness in state affairs. He knew not why, but he feared for the Duke should he put too much faith in the chancellor, for he thought he could read intrigue and falsehood in his eye.

Just as he saw the hump and flowing yellow cloak turn the corner at the end of the gallery, a voice whispered to him: "Don't trust that yellow-faced hypocrite!" It was the fifer of Hardt, who had stolen to his side unnoticed.

"How! are you there, Hans?" cried Albert, and gladly proffered his hand. "Are you come to the castle to visit us? that's very kind; you are more heartily welcome than that humpbacked knave; but what have you to say of him that I should beware of?"

"He is a false man, and I have warned the Duke not to follow his advice, which made him very angry with me. He puts his whole confidence in him."

"But what did he say? Have you seen him this morning?" asked Albert.

"I went to take my leave of him, for I am going home to my wife and child. The Duke appeared moved at first, spoke of the days of his exile, and asked me to mention any act of grace he could confer upon me. But I merited none, for what I have done for him was only paying off an old debt. I asked him at last, not being able to think of anything else, to allow me the liberty to shoot my fox without being punished as a poacher. He laughed, and said I might do it, but that was no act of grace, I must demand something else. Well, I took courage, and said, I beg of your grace not to put too much confidence in the crafty chancellor, for it is my opinion he is false at heart."

"That's just what I think," cried Albert; "he looked as if he wanted to spy into my most inward thoughts with those green eyes of his; but what answered the Duke?"

"'You understand nothing upon such subjects,' was his reply, and became angry; and added, 'you may be a faithful and sure guide among clefts and caverns, but the chancellor understands state intrigues better than you.' It may be," added the fifer, "that I am wrong in my conjectures; I hope so, for the Duke's sake. So now farewell, sir; may God protect you! Amen."

"Will you really go, and not remain for my wedding?" said Albert. "I expect the knight of Lichtenstein and his daughter here to-day. Stay a day or two longer: you were our messenger of love, and ought not to desert us at this happy moment."

"Of what use can a poor man like me be at the wedding of a knight? I might, indeed, sit among the musicians, and take part in the music in honour of the happy event; but others can do it as well as me, and my house requires my presence."

"Well then, farewell," said Albert; "give my salutations to your wife and Barbelle, and visit us often in Lichtenstein. God be with you!"

A tear filled the eye of the young man as he gave the peasant a hearty parting shake of the hand, for he had always found him an honest trustworthy man, a faithful servant of the Duke, a bold companion in danger, and cheerful society in misfortune. He was about asking many questions concerning the mysterious life which this man followed, for he was particularly curious to know the cause of his extraordinary attachment to the Duke, but he suppressed them out of delicacy to his feelings. The natural greatness of mind which characterised the fifer of Hardt, though he were a common peasant, awed him into silence touching those subjects which his friend had always appeared to wish to avoid.

"But, I have one thing more to say," said Hans, as he was going: "do you know that your old friend and future cousin-in-law, von Kraft, is here?"

"The scribe to the council? how did he come here? he's a Leaguist!"

"He is here, nevertheless, and not in the most agreeable position--for he is in prison. Yesterday evening, when the people assembled in the market place, in consequence of the Duke's arrival, it appears he addressed them in favour of the League."

"Good heavens!" exclaimed Albert, "was that Dieterich Kraft, the scribe? I must go instantly to the Duke, who now sits in judgment upon him, or the chancellor will have his head off. Good bye!"

The young man hurried along the corridor to the Duke's apartment. He had been in the habit in Mömpelgard of having immediate access to him at all times of day, and, therefore, the porter now respectfully opened the door. He entered in a hasty manner, to the astonishment of the Duke, who was somewhat displeased; but the chancellor masked his hypocrisy, as usual, under a smile of mildness.

"Good morning, Sturmfeder," said the Duke, who sat at a table, dressed in a green coat embroidered in gold, with a green hunting cap on his head; "I hope you have slept well in our castle. What brings you thus early to us? we have important business."

The eyes of the young man had in the mean time anxiously looked about the room, and there discovered the scribe of the Ulmer council standing in a corner. He was as pale as death; his hair, which was wont to be combed with great care, hung in disorder over his neck, and a rose-coloured gown which he wore over a black coat was torn to tatters. His eyes met Albert's with a most pitiable look, and he then glanced upwards, as much as to say, "it is all over with me." Near him stood other men: one of whom, tall and meagre, he thought to have seen before. The prisoners were guarded by Peter, the brave Magdeburger, and Staberl of Vienna. They stood at their post with outstretched legs, their halberds resting on the floor, upright as candles.

"I say, we have important business at present," continued the Duke; "but why do you look so intent upon him with the rose-coloured gown? he is a hardened sinner; the sword is being sharpened for his neck!"

"Will your highness allow me but one word," replied Albert. "I know that man, and would stake all I possess in the world, that he is a peaceable subject; and positively not a criminal who deserves death."

"By Saint Hubertus, that is a bold speech! You have changed your nature, methinks: my chancellor, the worthy jurist, has put himself forward like a young warrior; and you, my young soldier, would assume the advocate. What say you to that, Ambrosius Bolland?"

"Hi! hi! I adorned my person by way of letting your highness have a joke, for I know, of old date, you are fond of a little fun; and our dear good Sturmfeder, for the sake of adding to it, plays the part of a jurist. Hi! hi! hi! but all he may say or do, he cannot save him in the rose-coloured gown. High treason! he must lose his head, poor fellow!"

"Mr. Chancellor," cried Albert, glowing with anger, "the Duke can witness, that I was never accustomed to play the buffoon. I don't wish to rival any person in this sort of character; but I never play or make sport with the life of a fellow creature! I am seriously in earnest, when I pledge my life for the noble Dieterich von Kraft, scribe to the council of Ulm, now present before you. I hope my bail will be taken."

"How?" said Ulerich, "is he the elegant gentleman, your host in Ulm, of whom you have often spoke to me. I regret that he committed himself so far as to be taken in the act of creating an insurrection, under very suspicious circumstances."

"Certainly," croaked Ambrosius, "a *crimen lesæ majestatis!*"

"Permit me, sir, to speak," said Albert. "I have studied law long enough to know, that in this case it is absurd to talk of treason. The governor and council of the League were still in the town last night, consequently Stuttgardt was in the power of the enemy, and the scribe, who is in no wise a subject of his highness, did not act differently from any other Leaguist soldier, who takes the field against the Duke by the orders of his superiors."

"Ei, youth, youth! How nicely it accommodates itself to circumstances!" said the chancellor; "but my worthy friend, you must know that so soon as the Duke summoned the town, and had the *animum possidentis,* every thing within its walls belonged to him. Therefore, any conspiracy against his royal person, becomes high treason immediately. The prisoner Dieterich von Kraft held very dangerous language to the people."

"Impossible! it is quite contrary to his manner and principles. My Lord Duke, it cannot be!"

"Albert!" said the Duke in earnest, "we have had much patience in hearing what you have to say; but it can do your friend no good. Here is the protocol. The chancellor had examined witnesses before I came, and every thing is proved as clear as day. We must make an example. The chancellor is perfectly right; therefore I cannot hold out any act of grace in the prisoner's favour."

"But allow me to ask him and the witnesses one question--only a few words," said Albert.

"That is against all forms of justice," said the chancellor; "I must protest against it; it is an infringement on my office."

"Let it be, Ambrosius," said the Duke. "He may ask a question, with all my heart, of the poor sinner, who has no chance of escape."

"Dieterich von Kraft," said Albert, addressing the prisoner, "how came you to be in Stuttgardt?"

The forlorn scribe, whom death seemed already to have made his prey, turning his eyes towards him, his teeth chattering from fear, was scarcely able to mutter a word in answer. "I was sent here by the council of Ulm, as secretary to the governor."

"How was it that you appeared before the burghers of Stuttgardt, yesterday evening?" said Albert.

"The governor ordered me to remind them of their duty and oath, should there, perchance, be an insurrection against the League."

"Don't you perceive, he was only acting under orders?" said Albert, turning to the Duke. "Who took you prisoner?" he continued with the examination.

"The man standing beside you."

"Did you take this gentleman into custody? then you must have heard what he said; what did he say?" said Albert to the man.

"Yes, I heard what he said," answered the burgher; "he had spoken but six words, when burghermaster Hartmann threw him down from the bank. I remember what they were, namely: 'Recollect, my friends, what will the illustrious council of the League say!' That was all, and then Hartmann took him by the collar. But there stands Doctor Calmus, who made a longer speech."

The Duke roared with laughter, first looking at Albert and then at the chancellor, who turned pale, and was so disconcerted, that he could scarcely muster up courage to join in his master's hilarity. "Were those all the dangerous words he spoke--is this the charge of high treason--'What would the council of the League say?' Poor Kraft! These few words have brought your neck within a hair's breadth of the executioner's sword. We have often heard our friends say, 'What will folks think, when they hear the Duke is in the country again?' therefore, I will not punish him. What think you of it, Sturmfeder?"

"I know not what reason you could have had," said Albert, addressing the chancellor, with anger beaming in his eyes, "to have pushed the case to such lengths, and advised the Duke to these harsh measures; which, instead of healing past grievances, would only cause the cry of 'tyrant' to be raised everywhere against him. If you have acted from an overheated zeal of duty, you have this once surpassed the bounds of discretion."

The chancellor was silent, and satisfied himself by throwing a furious glance at the young man. The Duke stood up, and said, "You must not blame my little adviser for his zeal in my cause, which has perhaps made him act with too much severity in this instance. There, take your rose-coloured friend with you, give him a glass to expel his ghastly fear, and then let him go wherever he will. And you, dog of a doctor, as for you, who are not worthy of the title of dog doctor, a Würtemberg gallows is too good for you. You will be hung one of these days, so I will not give myself the trouble to do it at present. Long Peter, order your men to bind that fellow on an ass, with his face to the tail, and lead him through the town, and thence let him be sent to Esslingen, to his wise counsellors, to whom he and his beast belong. Away with him!"

The features of the wretched doctor, who had hitherto sat in fear of death, soon cheered up by this happy change in his fate; he breathed more freely, and made a low bow. Peter, Staberl, and the Magdeburger, laid hold of him with savage joy, hoisted him on their broad shoulders, and bore him away.

The scribe of Ulm shed tears of joy, and, impelled by gratitude, wanted to kiss the Duke's cloak; but he turned away, and waved to Albert to withdraw his friend.

CHAPTER XXIX

Stop! stay thy hand, and hear my prayer,--
Ah, do not let it be:
You cannot, must not, will not dare
A deed unworthy thee.

Schiller.

The scribe of the grand council of Ulm did not appear to have sufficiently recovered from his state of terror to answer the many questions his preserver put to him as they passed along the passages and galleries. He trembled in all his limbs, his knees shook, and he often looked back with a feeling of apprehension, lest the Duke should have repented of his act of grace, and the unmerciful chancellor in the yellow gown should sneak after him, and suddenly pounce upon him. Having reached Albert's apartment, he sank exhausted in a chair, and it was some time before he could collect his thoughts to be able to answer his friend.

"Your politics, cousin, had well nigh played you a sorry trick," said Albert; "but what possessed you to set yourself up as a popular speaker in Stuttgardt? And, above all, how could you think of quitting your comfortable establishment in Ulm, the assiduous care of your old nurse Sabina, and fly the vicinity of the charming Marie, to come here in the service of the governor?"

"Ah! she it was who sent me into the jaws of death; she is the cause of all my trouble. Ah! that I had never left my dear Ulm! All my misfortunes began with my first step over our boundary."

"Did Marie persuade you?" Albert asked; "have you not succeeded in the object of your desires? Has she discarded you, and did you out of desparation--"

"God forbid! Marie is as good as my bride; that's my calamity. When you left Ulm, I had a dispute with Mrs. Sabina, the nurse which determined me to demand Marie's hand of my uncle. I was accepted; but, the girl's head being completely turned by your military mania, nothing would satisfy her but that I must first encounter the dangers and hardships of a campaign, and become a man like you. Not until then would she marry me. Oh, merciful Heaven!"

"So now you are formally in the field against Würtemberg? What a bold spirit that girl has!"

"Yes, I am in the field; I shall never in my life forget what I have gone through! My old John and I were obliged to march with the army of the League. What pain and trouble? often compelled to ride eight hours a day. My dress was disordered, everything full of dust and filth; my coat of mail squeezed me to death. I could stand it no longer; and as old John ran back to Ulm, I asked for a place as writer on the staff, hired a litter and two stout horses to carry my baggage, which made my case more bearable."

"Then you were carried into the field like dogs to the hunt," said Albert. "Have you been in an action?"

"Oh! yes; at Tübingen, I was in the thick of it. Not twenty paces from me a man was killed as dead as a mouse. I shall never forget the fright I was in, if I live eighty years. After we had perfectly subdued the whole country, I was appointed to the honourable situation of secretary to the governor in Stuttgardt. We lived quietly, and in peace, until the restless Duke returned once more to disturb us. Oh! had I but followed my own wish, and joined the representatives of the League at Nördlingen! but I feared the fatigue of the journey."

"But why did you not depart with the governor when we arrived? He is now quietly seated in Esslingen, until we hunt him out of it."

"He deserted us shamefully," said Kraft; "and intrusted everything to my head, which has nearly suffered for it. I had not the least idea the danger was so imminent, and allowed myself to be seduced by Doctor Calmus to speak to the people, and warn them against breaking their oath to the League. Had I but succeeded, it would have made a noise in the world, and I should have stood high in Marie's estimation. But the Würtembergers are barbarians, and void of all decent manners. They did not even let me say a word, but threw me down, and treated me like a common vagabond. Just look at my cloak, it is torn to tatters! I regret it, for it cost me four gold florins, and Marie maintains that rose colour becomes the complexion of my face to perfection."

Albert scarcely knew whether to laugh at the folly of his friend the scribe, or admire the stoical composure with which he lamented his torn gown, when he had but a moment before narrowly escaped losing his head. He was going to ask some other questions about his adventures, when an extraordinary noise was heard under the window in the open space before the castle; he looked out, and beckoned to Dieterich von Kraft to come and witness a spectacle of fallen greatness.

Doctor Calmus was being paraded through the town. He was seated on an ass, with his face towards the tail. The lansquenets had dressed him out in a ridiculous manner, with a painted leather cap, at the top of which was stuck a large cock's feather. Two drummers led the procession, on either side, the Magdeburger, Staberl of Vienna, the late Captain Muckerle, and the brave general, marched with solemn pace, every now and then pricking the animal with the ends of their halberts to quicken his pace. An immense crowd of people swarmed around him, pelting him with eggs and mud.

The scribe looked down upon his unfortunate companion in distress with pity, and sighed, "It's hard to be obliged to ride upon an ass in that fashion, but it's better than being hanged." He turned from the scene, and looked towards another side of the square. "Who comes here?" he asked the young knight; "that's just the kind of thing I went to the field in."

His friend looked round, and perceived a train of travellers with a litter in the middle. An old man on horseback brought up the rear of the party, which now moved towards the castle. Albert observing them more closely, cried out, in wild joy, "It's them! it's them! it is her father, and she is in the litter!" One spring took him out of the room, to the great astonishment of the scribe. "Who can it be? what father?" said he. He returned to the window, and looking out, he saw the cavalcade stop on the drawbridge, and in the same moment his friend fly through the gate. Dieterich then observed him to open the door like a madman, a lady in a veil stepped out of the litter, and when she threw it back, to his great surprise he recognised his cousin Bertha von Lichtenstein. "But only see; he kisses her in the public street," said the scribe to himself, shaking his head, "I have never seen such joy before! But, alas! there goes the father to the litter; what angry eyes he will make! how he will stamp and swear! but no, he nods kindly to my friend; he dismounts, he embraces him.--Well, that's very curious, I must say!"

The scribe could scarcely believe his eyes, and to convince himself that he was not deceived, left the room, and went into the gallery, where he perceived the old knight of Lichtenstein coming up the stairs, leading Albert by his right hand, and Cousin Bertha by the left. He thought a great alteration for the better had taken place in her beautiful features, since the time they had made such a deep impression on his heart, and still lived in his recollection.

He had seen her for the first time in Ulm, when she appeared to him like a messenger from a fairy land, so dignified was the expression of her eyes, majesty sat upon her brow, and her whole countenance bespoke a mind far above the common stamp of mortals. The scribe had often puzzled his mind in the attempt to unravel the mystery by which she had gained such influence over him. The damsels of Ulm possessed perhaps cheeks fresher and more plump, eyes more lively, a more attractive smile, and perhaps greater brilliancy of youth. But there was a something in Bertha which he could not account for, which inspired him with awe. Was it the dark eyelashes, which, like a veil, fell over her eyes, and concealed the starting tear? Was it the delicately compressed lip, upon which was encamped the expression of painful grief? or the rapid change of colour upon her features, which appeared to betray suffering of some acute feeling--perhaps of love? Marie's cheerfulness, her easy manners, a certain art of teasing, which imparted life and good will to all around her, had long since driven her cousin's image from his heart; but now that he came again in contact with the influence of the lady of Lichtenstein, poor Dieterich von Kraft felt all his old wounds bleed afresh. What was the power which worked in so different a manner upon his feelings was a question beyond his comprehension. Though there was the same dignity, the same expression, which commands the respect and admiration of the beholder, her eye was now animated with placid joy, a pleasing smile played on her lips, and her cheeks bloomed with unalloyed happiness. Dieterich von Kraft had made these observations in speechless astonishment, when the old knight first noticed him. "Do my eyes deceive me?" he cried, "Dieterich von Kraft, my nephew! What brings you to Stuttgardt? Perhaps you come to the wedding of my daughter with Albert von Sturmfeder? But how you look! What's the matter with you? How pale and miserable your whole appearance, and your clothes hang about your body all in rags! What has happened?"

The scribe eyed his rose-coloured gown in despair and dismay, and blushed; "God knows!" he said, "I am ashamed to shew myself before any decent person. These cursed Würtembergers, these vine-dressers and contemptible shoemakers, have mangled me in this way. Verily, and in truth, the whole illustrious League has been attacked and insulted in my individual person!"

"You ought to be thankful, cousin, that it was no worse," said Albert, as he led the travellers into his apartment; "only think, father, last night, when we stood before the gates, he was exciting the burghers to rebellion against us, for which the chancellor wanted to have his head this morning. It was with very great difficulty I could persuade the Duke to pardon him; and now he complains of the Würtembergers having torn his cloak."

"With your gracious permission," said Mrs. Rosel, the old nurse, and curtsied three times to the scribe, "if my assistance is agreeable, I'll mend the gown, so that you shall not know it has been torn. The proverb says,

'If the young man his new gown has torn,

The old woman can mend it fit to be worn.'"

Dieterich von Kraft accepted the offer with many thanks. He retired to a window with old Rosel, when she pulled out of her large leather pocket all the necessary articles for the purpose of repairing his damages. She entertained him upon the inexhaustible subject of housekeeping, particularly upon the important science of dressing certain dishes not to be found in Mrs. Sabina's catalogue of cookery. At a distance from this couple, at the other end of the room, sat Bertha and Albert, engaged in the confidential whisperings of love. Neither Johannes Thethingerus, nor Johannes Bezius, neither Gabelkofer nor Crusius, though we have to thank them for much important information of old times, have mentioned what these two lovers had to say to each other on that morning. Thus much we know, however, that satisfaction rested upon Bertha's features, expressive of her joy at the near approach of the happy moment to complete her union with Albert.

The reader will thank us if we lead him from a scene of so little historical interest, and of which every one is supposed to know more or less, to follow the path of the knight of Lichtenstein. Having left his daughter to the care of Albert, and his nephew to the ingenious hand of Mrs. Rosel, he himself repaired to the apartment of the Duke. Age had imprinted on his countenance an air of gravity, which at this hour appeared to have received an additional stamp of painful thought, amounting almost to despondency. This man had inherited his love for the house of Würtemberg from his ancestors. Habit and inclination had bound him to the sovereigns who had presided over Würtemberg during the course of his long life. The misfortunes and calumnies which, had been heaped upon Ulerich, had not had the effect of shaking the faithful heart of the old man in the Duke's cause. On the contrary, they tended only to draw the ties of friendship tighter. With the joy of a bridegroom who hastens to the wedding, and with the strength and vivacity of youth, he undertook the long and fatiguing journey from his castle to Stuttgardt, when he heard the Duke had taken Leonberg, and had advanced to the capital. Having entertained no doubt of the Duke's success, he was not deceived in his calculation, and he arrived at Stuttgardt the morning after the establishment of the new authority.

The news which Albert imparted to him as they proceeded up stairs, was not calculated to excite the joy of the old man. "The Duke," he whispered to him, "the Duke does not appear to be inclined to act with prudence; God knows what his intentions may be respecting the government of the country, for he let fall some extraordinary sentiments on the road, which I fear will not be improved in the hands of his chancellor, Ambrosius Bolland." The mere mention of this name was sufficient to raise great uneasiness in the breast of the knight of Lichtenstein. He was acquainted with Bolland; and though he knew him to be expert, and particularly well versed in state affairs, and capable of executing any intricate piece of service, yet he was a man who had often played a deep, if not a false game. "Should the Duke give his confidence to this man, and follow his council, may God be merciful to him! The country is a mere bit of parchment in the eyes of Ambrosius, to be turned and twisted according to his whim. He'll know how to shape and fashion it preparatory to meeting the Duke's eye; but he'll keep the pen in his own hand. But, as old Rosel would say, 'Any fool can cut out; the art is to sew the garment together.'" Thus thought the knight of Lichtenstein, in passing along the gallery. He seized his long white beard in anger; whilst his heart beat with zeal in the cause of Würtemberg.

He was immediately admitted to the presence of the Duke, whom he found in deep; consultation with Ambrosius. The latter was seated, holding a large swan's pen in one hand and a parchment in the other, which was written over with black, red, and blue ink, in many neat columns. The Duke was playing with a piece of sealing wax, which he held in his hand; and appeared in a state of indecision, first casting a penetrating glance at the chancellor, and then looking at the wax, as if it were destined to seal some important document. They were both so deeply immersed in their occupation, that Lichtenstein stood some minutes in the room, contemplating with intense interest the noble features of the Duke, without being remarked. The various sensations which were agitating him were plainly visible upon his countenance and in his expressive eyes. The frown upon his forehead, giving place in rapid succession to a milder expression, bespoke a mind hesitating between an act of severity and one of grace, whilst his companion, presenting him with the pen which he held in his hand, sat before him like the tempter. He turned and moved about like the serpent; and the eternal hypocritical smile, which his little green eyes could with ease convert into the expression of humility when his master looked at him sharply, appeared to urge him to taste the forbidden fruit.

"I cannot comprehend," said the chancellor with an insinuating tone of voice, "why your Grace will not do it! Did Cæsar hesitate to pass the Rubicon? A great man must use strong measures. The present age and futurity will laud your courage in having burst asunder the chains which now bind your hands."

"Are you so sure of that, Ambrosius Bolland?" replied the Duke, with a look of doubt. "Will it not be said, Duke Ulerich was a tyrant: he abrogated the old order of things, which was held sacred by his forefathers; and, having broken the contract which he himself established, treated his country as an enemy, and trod under foot the laws which----"

"Permit me," interrupted the other: "the only question is, who is to be master--the Duke or the country? If the country is to govern, the case is different; for then pacts, contracts, clauses, and such like, are necessary. The nobles, clergy, and commons, would be the masters, and your grace--a mere cypher; but if you hold the reins in your own hand, and wield your own will unrestricted, from that moment you become the source of all law. The sword is now in your hand,--you are lord and master; therefore, away with the old law--here is a new one--take the pen, and, in God's name, sign."

The Duke remained some time in doubtful suspense, agitated between conflicting struggles of conscience. At length, as if impelled by some evil genius, he said, "Am not I Würtemberg itself? the country and laws are concentrated in my person--I will sign!" He stretched out his hand to receive the pen from the chancellor, when he felt his arm arrested. He looked around in surprise, and met the placid but stern eye of the knight of Lichtenstein.

"Ha! welcome, my faithful Lichtenstein; I will be ready to speak with you instantly, only let me sign this parchment."

"Allow me, your grace," said the old man: "having promised me a voice in your council, may I look at the first ordinance which you are about to issue to your country."

"With your most noble permission," said Ambrosius Holland, hastily, "delay were dangerous: the citizens of Stuttgardt are already assembled, and it is requisite to read the proclamation without loss of time."

"The thing is not so very pressing, after all," said the Duke, "that we cannot impart the contents to our friend. We have accordingly determined," he added, addressing Lichtenstein, "to administer a new oath of fidelity, making the people swear allegiance to us, under a fresh contract and different laws. The old ones are null and void from henceforth."

"Is that your determination?" replied the knight of Lichtenstein; "and have you maturely considered what will be the consequences of this act? Did you not swear but a few years ago to the Tübingen compact?"

"Tübingen!" cried the Duke with a terrible voice, his eyes flashing the fire of indignation; "Tübingen! mention that word no more! In that vile city were centred all my hopes, my country, my children,--ha! and on that spot was I betrayed and sold. I begged, I implored them to hold out to the last; I was ready to share my property, my blood with them in its defence; but no! they would not hear of Ulerich, nor listen to his voice. They preferred the new order of things; they suffered me to linger in the misery of banishment, and caused the name of Würtemberg to become the contempt and derision of all the world. But now that I am lord and master again, with my sword in my hand, I'll not allow it to be wrenched a second time from my grasp. If they have forgotten their oath, by Saint Hubertus, my memory is also equally treacherous. The Tübingen compact, did you say? May dire necessity confound every thing connected with that name!"

"But recollect, your grace!" said Lichtenstein, staggered at this burst of passion; "think of the impression such a step will make throughout the country. At this moment you have only Stuttgardt and its neighbourhood in your possession; whereas Urach, Asperg, Tübingen, and Göppingen, have all Leaguist garrisons. Will the country people; stand by you to drive them out, when they become acquainted with the new ordinance to which they are to swear allegiance?"

"I maintain it," said the Duke; "did the country stand by me when I was forced to turn my back upon Würtemberg? No! they saw me hunted down like a wild beast, and sided with the League!"

"Pardon me, my Lord Duke," replied the old man; "but that is not the case. I recollect well that day in Blaubeuren. Who held to you on that occasion, when the Swiss deserted you? who implored you not to leave the country? who offered to sacrifice their lives in your cause? It was eight thousand Würtembergers! Have you forgotten that day?"

"Ay-ay! most worthy sir," said the chancellor, who was aware what an impression these remarks were likely to make on Ulerich; "ay! but that's nothing to the purpose. Besides, we have not to legislate upon what took place at that time, but upon the actual state of affairs. The country has completely absolved itself of the former oath, by swearing allegiance to the usurpations of the League. His grace is now to be considered in the light of a new Lord, having subdued the country by force of arms; and, therefore, as the League instituted their own peculiar measures, the Duke has a right to follow their example. A new Lord gives new laws. He has the privilege at all times to govern according to his own will and pleasure. Shall I dip the pen in the ink, gracious sir?"

"Sir Chancellor!" said Lichtenstein, with a determined voice, "though I have all possible respect for your learning and foresight, you advance that which is positively false, and your counsel is dangerous. The question now is, to ascertain who it is that the people love. The League, by their violent measures, have estranged the public mind from them; this was therefore precisely the most favourable moment for the Duke to appear in the country, for all hearts are with him; but if you repel the good feeling of the people by insidious measures, if you attempt to destroy the ancient laws and institutions, and build upon their ruins your own invented constitution, oh, beware! beware of the consequences, and remember that the love of the people is the only powerful support upon which you can rely."

The Duke stood with folded arms, deep in thought, and made no answer. With so much more warmth did the chancellor reply: "Hi! hi! hi! where did you concoct that pretty little speech, my most worthy and highly honoured sir? Love of the people, did you say? The Romans, in their day, knew very well what that meant. Nothing but soap bubbles, soap bubbles! I thought you possessed more acuteness. To whom does the country belong? Here! here stands Würtemberg, personified in the Duke! it belongs to him, he has inherited it; and besides which, he has now conquered it. The people's love? Bah! it resembles April weather! Had it been so strong as you talk of, would they have sworn allegiance to the League?"

"The Chancellor is right!" cried the Duke, starting from his thoughtful mood. "You may mean well, Lichtenstein, but this once you are in the wrong. It was my forbearance which caused me to be driven from my country; now that I am returned, they shall feel that I am the master. The pen, Chancellor;--I say, it's my will and pleasure, and they shall obey!"

"Oh! my Lord!" said Lichtenstein, "do not commit yourself in the heat of passion: wait till your blood cools. Assemble the states, make any alterations in the constitution you may think proper--only not at this moment--not as long as the League possesses a foot of land in Würtemberg. This rash act may prejudice your cause. Consent to a short delay."

"Indeed!" interrupted the chancellor, "and let them by degrees come round to the old state of things? Do you suppose, when once the representatives are assembled and talk over their affairs, they will concede to your reform with good will? Hi! hi! force will be requisite to compel them, and that's what will create hatred. Strike the iron whilst it's hot. Or is it your grace's pleasure, to stand again humbly under the yoke, and be forced to bend to circumstances?"

The Duke did not answer, but snatching the pen and parchment impatiently out of the chancellor's hands, cast a hasty and penetrating look, first at him and then at the knight, and, before the latter could hinder him, signed his name. Old Lichtenstein remained in speechless consternation; his head sunk over his breast. The chancellor glanced a triumphant look at him and at the Duke. Ulerich seized a silver hand-bell, which was on the table, and rang violently. A page entered, and asked his commands.

"Are the citizens assembled?" asked the Duke.

"Yes, your grace! they are assembled on the meadow near to Cannstadt. Six companies of the lansquenet also are moving in that direction."

"The lansquenet! Who ordered them?"

The chancellor trembled when he heard this last question. "It was only for the sake of keeping order," said he, "I thought of it, because in such cases it is generally the custom to have armed men by way of precaution----"

The Duke waved to him to be silent. An expression in the look of the knight condemnatory of this rash act, met the Duke's eye, and caused him to blush. "It has been done without my permission," said he; "but----if we now recall them, it would create suspicion. However, it is of no great consequence. Bring me my red cloak and hat;--quick!"

The Duke stept to the window, and looked out in silence. The chancellor appeared uncertain whether his master was angry or not, and did not venture to speak; whilst the knight of Lichtenstein continued wrapt in deep anxious thought. They remained some time in this state, until the entrance of attendants interrupted the silence. Four pages entered the apartment, one carrying the cloak, another the hat, a third a gold chain, and the fourth the military sword of the Duke. They robed him in his ducal mantle of purple velvet, trimmed with ermine. His hat was then presented to him, carrying the black and yellow colours of the house of Würtemberg in rich waving plumes, bound together by a clasp of gold, set in precious stones, the value of which was worth a seigniory. The Duke covered his head with his hat. His powerful figure appeared more dignified in this dress than it did before, and his open majestic forehead, with his brilliant eye sparkling from beneath the flowing feathers, inspired awe in those around him. He desired the pages to place the gold chain over his neck; then, buckling on his sword, gave a sign to the chancellor to follow.

The knight of Lichtenstein still uttered not a word. He had observed these preparations with a troubled countenance, and turned away from the scene. The Duke made a slight inclination of the head to his old friend as he passed him in going towards the door, followed by the strange figure of the Chancellor Ambrosius Bolland, who strutted with magisterial step. He did not think it necessary to salute the old man, his master not having done so, but satisfied his malice by casting a crafty triumphant look at the spot where he was standing, accompanied by a scornful smile, which played about his toothless mouth. The Duke stopt on the threshold of the door, and, looking back, his better nature appeared to get the mastery of him; he returned to Lichtenstein, to the astonishment and confusion of the chancellor.

"Old man, and faithful friend," said he, trying in vain to conceal a deep emotion which agitated him, "you were my only friend in my troubles, and I have experienced your tried fidelity on a hundred different occasions,--proofs sufficient to convince me of your attachment to Würtemberg. I feel this step the most important of my life, and, perhaps, the most hazardous; but where the stake is high we must risk the more."

The knight of Lichtenstein raised his venerable head, with tears in his eyes. He seized Ulerich's hand, and said, "Remain, for God's sake! follow my advice only this once! My hair is grey,--I have lived long, and known and loved you since your thirteenth year." At this moment the drums of the lansquenet sounded in the courtyard, the impatient stamping of horses echoed through the vaulted halls, and the heralds blew their trumpets to proclaim the taking the oath of fidelity.

"Jacta alea esto! was Cæsar's motto," said the Duke, with animated countenance. "I am now going to cross my Rubicon. But give me your blessing, old man,--advice is too late."

The knight cast his eyes around, evidently suffering from intense agony; his voice refused utterance to his feelings, and he pressed the Duke's right hand to his heart in token of bestowing his blessing. The chancellor, observing a momentary hesitation in the Duke to quit his friend, stretched forth his long withered arm from under his cloak, and pointed to the roll of parchment. He looked like the tempter who had succeeded in dragging another victim after him in chains. Ulerich von Würtemberg tore himself away, and went to hear the oath of allegiance administered.

CHAPTER XXX

No furnace ever blazed so bright,
Nor glow'd the burning brand
With half so powerful a light,
As love of fatherland.

An old popular Song.

The apprehensions of the knight of Lichtenstein were not so totally void of foundation as Ambrosius Bolland had represented them to be. A large portion of the country had, indeed, joined the Duke, arising partly from, the predilection of the people in favour of the hereditary house of Würtemberg, but in a great measure from the oppressions of the League, who had forcibly compelled them to submit to their rule. Many were, at first, induced to join his standard, and declare for Würtemberg, when they heard that victory followed Ulerich's path; but the new oath of allegiance, by which all ancient laws were to be abrogated, and the report that the refractory were to be compelled by force to subscribe to these forms, had the effect, at least, of not adding to the Duke's popularity,--a defect, in such doubtful undertakings as the present, often felt too late to be remedied. Urach, Göppingen, and Tübingen were still in the hands of the League, having powerful garrisons in each. Dieterich Spät, the Duke's bitterest enemy, was established in Urach. He recruited so many men in a few days, that he not only kept his district in subjection, but was enabled to make incursions into the country which had submitted to the Duke. The report was also spread that the assembly of the League at Nördlingen had separated, each member hurrying home to re-organize a fresh army to meet Ulerich a second time in the field.

The Duke, in the meanwhile, appeared nowise concerned in the midst of the unsettled state of the country. Ambrosius Bolland was his sole counsellor, with whom he transacted business with closed doors. Many messengers were observed to arrive and depart, but no one could learn what was going on. Judging from the Duke's cheerful mood, it was thought in Stuttgardt that affairs were in a prosperous state; for when he rode through the streets, followed by a brilliant suite, saluting all the pretty females, and joking and laughing with his attendants who rode by his side, every one said, "Duke Ulerich is as merry as he was before the days of 'the Poor

Conrad insurrection.'" He established his court in its former magnificence. Though it was no longer the point of reunion of the Bavarian, Swabian, and Franconian counts and nobles, nor the gay assemblage of princesses who formerly attracted such a splendid train of blooming beauties around them, there was still no lack of handsome women and gay-dressed knights to adorn his court. The atmosphere of the town appeared also to impart additional lustre to the beauties of Stuttgardt at that time, for, when they congregated in the saloons and halls of the castle, the assembly had more the character of a select choice of the fairest belles of the land than one of ordinary occurrence.

The dance and tournament were re-established in all their former spirit. Feast followed feast in such rapid succession that Ulerich seemed to wish to make up for the time he had lost in the misery of banishment. Not the least of these gay doings was the wedding of Albert von Sturmfeder with the heiress of Lichtenstein.

The old knight was some time before he could make up his mind to put his promise into execution, not that he had any objection to the choice of his daughter, for he loved his future son-in-law with the affection of a father; he even felt his younger days revive again as it were in his own person, and could not forget the disinterested sacrifice Albert had made in sharing the exile of the Duke; but, like as the horizon of Ulerich's affairs was enveloped in darkness, so was the old man's brow clouded by anxious misgivings, apprehensive lest circumstances should not long remain in the state they were. He was deeply hurt also that the Duke, who gave his confidence exclusively to the crafty chancellor, did not admit him to his council in the many weighty matters now in agitation. Indecision and anxiety of mind, had caused him to put off the day of joy; but, moved by the expressive eyes of his daughter, in which he thought to read a gentle reproach, and the entreaties of Albert, he at last consented to their importunities, and fixed a day, to which the Duke acquiesced; but would allow of no one making the necessary arrangements for the wedding but himself. Amidst the success which had hitherto attended him, Ulerich did not forget those nights when old Lichtenstein proved his attachment to him by his assiduous attention to his wants, and when the delicate frame of his daughter braved storm and cold to receive him at the gate of the castle, and prepare warm food to cheer him when he came from the cavern. Neither was the sacrifice which the bridegroom had made for his sake obliterated from his memory. His noble mind was fully alive to the fidelity, love, and sacrifices they had each so fully manifested, and, therefore, he wished to prove his sense of gratitude to them. The knight and his daughter had hitherto been his guests at the castle. He now completely furnished a house for them near the collegiate church, and, on the evening before the nuptials, he delivered the key of it to the lady of Lichtenstein, begging her to make use of it whenever she came to Stuttgardt.

The day at length arrived,--a day which Albert had once thought far distant, but to which his most longing desire had ever been, constantly directed. When he rose on that morning he recalled to his mind all the circumstances which had happened to him since his heart had been engaged, and was astonished to think how differently things had come to pass to what he could have at first imagined. Who would ever have supposed, when he rode through the beech wood towards his home, that the happiness of possessing his beloved Bertha was not so distant as he then had reason to fear? When he joined the League's army, in opposition to the Duke, the very last thing that could have entered his mind would have been that this same man, his enemy at that time, should be the instrument of completing his happiness! He could now contemplate in cheerful serenity the agitations of those days when he, with difficulty, stole a moment to whisper a word to his beloved for fear of her father, the avowed enemy of the League, And he thought of that hour in Marie's garden, the most painful he had ever experienced, when he took leave of Bertha, thinking she was lost to him for ever, whereas this day was to bind them eternally together. Every word she had ever spoken to him rushed to his recollection,--he was wrapped in admiration of her firm trust in Providence, who she was persuaded would order all things to work for their good. Though at that time their hopes, their prospects, were veiled in a dark uncertain futurity, she did not despond, but inspired her lover with courage when they took their parting embrace.

The train of these thoughts was interrupted by a modest tap at the door;--it was Dieterich von Kraft, who entered the room, dressed in his very best.

"How?" cried the scribe of the grand council of Ulm, and clasped his hands in astonishment,--"How? I hope you do not intend to be married in that jacket. It is nine o'clock already; the passages and stairs of the castle swarm with wedding guests, shining in silks and satins, and you, the principal performer in the piece, are looking unconcerned out of the window, instead of preparing yourself for the happy event?"

"There lies the whole concern," replied Albert, smiling, and pointing to his dress on the bed, "cap and feathers, mantle and jacket, all of the best quality and make; but God knows, I have not yet thought of hanging the tawdriness on my back. This jacket which I have on is dearer to me than all the rest; I have worn it in worse times, but still in very happy days."

"Yes, yes! I know it well; you wore it when you were with me in Ulm, and I don't forget how jealous Marie made me when she described it to me in glowing terms. But do you call that new dress tawdry? By Jove, I should be happy to possess such smart things the rest of my life! Only look at this white vest, embroidered in gold, and the blue velvet mantle: I have never seen anything more brilliant! truly, your choice has been made with great taste, and the dress matches the colour of your hair to perfection."

"The Duke presented me with it," said Albert, beginning to dress himself; "it would have been much too expensive for my slender finances."

"The Duke is really a splendid man; and now for the first time since I have been here do I perceive that we were too hard upon him in Ulm. There is some difference between life in such a city as this and that in our town. The court of the Duke of Würtemberg sounds much grander than the townhall of Ulm. Still I would not like to be in his skin; you'll see, cousin, his fortunes will go down-hill again with him."

"That's the burden of your old song, Dieterich: do you recollect how big you talked about your politics at that time in Ulm, expatiating how you intended to govern Würtemberg? How stands the case now?"

"Well, has it not turned out as I said?" replied the scribe, with a sagacious look; "I recollect, as if it were but yesterday, that I prophesied the Swiss would return home; that we should gain the hearts of the country people, and that the citizens would open the gates to us."

"Yes, yes! and you helped to accomplish all this," laughed Albert, "when you were carried to the field in a litter: but you also prophesied that the Duke would never be able to return to his country, and now you see he sits quietly and unmolested in his castle."

"Not so quiet as you may think. For your sake and his, I wish with all my heart he may hold his country. The war has done me no good, for the great men take everything for themselves, only leaving us subordinates the honour of having our heads cut off in the cause of the League. But though I wish him success, believe me, his affairs are not in the prosperous state you imagine. The governor and council who fled to Esslingen upon your arrival have petitioned the Emperor and Empire for assistance; the League is again in motion; and a fresh army is already assembling at Ulm."

"All talk,--nothing else," replied Albert; "I know for certain, that a reconciliation may take place between the Duke and Bavaria."

"Yes; but there is a great difference between *may* and *will* take place: thereby hangs many a difficult crotchet to unravel. But what do I see? you are not going to put that old rag of a scarf over your new wedding dress? they will not match together, my dear cousin."

The bridegroom regarded the scarf with a look of intense interest. "You don't understand," he replied, "why I set such a value upon it. It was Bertha's first present; she worked it secretly by night, in her room, when the news came that she was soon to leave Tübingen. It was my only consolation when I was absent from her, and therefore I will not fail to wear it on the happiest day of my life."

"Well, do as you please, in God's name, wear it! And now put on your cap, and be quick with the mantle, for they are beginning to ring the bells of the church. Beware of making the bride wait too long!"

The friendly scribe stood before the young man again, and minutely examined his dress with the eye of a connoisseur. He drew a buckle a little tighter here, he altered a plait of his mantle there, raised a feather of his cap higher, and having satisfied himself that nothing was wanting to adorn the person of the bridegroom, he thought his tall, manly figure, his fine head, and animated eye, were worthy the love of his pretty cousin. "I declare," said he, "you look as if you were created especially for a bridegroom. I would like Marie to see you now; poor girl, she would certainly be troubled with giddiness for a week! But come, come; I feel proud in being your companion upon this occasion, though I shall be fourteen days later in Ulm than I ought to be."

Albert blushed,--his heart beat quicker,--when he left the room. Joy, expectation, the fulfilment of year-long wishes assailed his feelings, as he followed his friend Dieterich through the galleries to the apartment where the assembled company awaited his arrival. The doors opened,--and Bertha stood in all the brilliancy of her beauty, surrounded by many women and maidens, whom the Duke had invited to form the nuptial procession.

When she perceived her lover enter the room, and met his glance, modest confusion spread a deep blush over her features, as she returned his salutation. The intoxicating joy of this moment would have led Albert to impress a morning salute of love upon her lips, but he was restrained by the strict manners of the times upon such occasions to observe a serious distant demeanour. A bride, according to etiquette, was not permitted to touch the hand of the bridegroom before the priest had joined them together, nor were they allowed to approach each other within six paces. To look even exclusively at her future husband before the ceremony was performed was deemed indecorous. She observed, therefore, the precise rule of remaining with cast-down looks, modest and demure, with her hands crossed before her. Such were the customs of the olden times of the country.

To any other person in a similar situation, the position in which she stood might have imparted to the beholder a stiff and awkward appearance;

but as nature endows her choicest daughters under all circumstances, whether in grief or joy, with a charm of interest which attracts even the most superficial observer, so did Bertha, on the present occasion, give to the restrained attitude of a bride in those days, an ease and grace which elicited the admiration of the surrounding spectators. The soft blush which rested on her features, the smile playing about her delicate-formed mouth, the brilliancy of her dark blue eyes, shooting their rays through the dark long eyelashes, like the rising sun dispersing the morning mist, formed a picture of unaffected loveliness, fit for the pencil of the artist.

The Duke entered the room, leading the knight of Lichtenstein by the hand. His eye rapidly passed through the circle of ladies, and he decidedly gave to Bertha the palm of beauty. "Sturmfeder," said he, taking him aside, "this day rewards you for many services. Do you recollect that night, when you first visited me in the cavern, and did not know who I was? Hans, the fifer, gave us a toast, 'the lady of Lichtenstein, long may she bloom for you!' she is yours now, and what is not less true, the toast you gave is also fulfilled, for we are again established in the castle of our fathers."

"May your grace enjoy your prosperity as long as I hope to be happy by the side of Bertha. But I am indebted to your interference and kindness for this day, for without it her father perhaps----"

"Honour for honour!" interrupted Ulerich: "you stood by us faithfully when we first set out to reconquer our country, and therefore we have assisted you in gaining possession of your best wishes. We will represent your father this day; and as such you will not refuse us to kiss your beautiful wife on the forehead after church."

Albert thought of that night when he was concealed behind the gate of Lichtenstein, and overheard the Duke's conversation with his love. It ended by his promise to remind her of his claim to a salute on this day, to which she would not consent then. "Where you please," he replied, "on her lips, if you prefer it, my Lord Duke; you have long since merited it by your generous intercession."

"Who is to accompany you to the altar?" said the Duke.

"Maxx Stumpf and the Ulmer scribe, a cousin of Lichtenstein."

"What, that smart little fellow, whose head my chancellor wanted to have off? Well, then, on your left you'll be supported by the most elegant of men; and on your right by the bravest in all Swabia. I wish you joy, young man; but take my advice, and lean to him on the right, rather than to the other; for if you have him for a friend, you need fear nothing in the world, even if you were as jealous as a Turk. But here comes the right one," he added, as the knight entered the room; "look how his broad sturdy figure shews among the crowd; and how splendidly he has dressed himself! He wore that old faded green mantle at our wedding with Sabina Lobesau, A.D. 1511."

"I don't understand much about dress," replied the brave knight of Schweinsberg, catching the Duke's last words, "neither do I know much about dancing, so you will excuse me; but if the bridegroom will break a lance with me this evening in a tilt, I am his man!"

"So you want to break a couple of his ribs out of pure tenderness and courtesy," said the Duke, laughing: "that's what I call a bridegroom's companion of the right sort. But stop, Albert; I would advise you to hold to your left-hand companion now, for the Ulmer will do you no harm."

The folding doors were at this instant thrown open; when the persons composing the Duke's court were seen stationed along the galleries. Pages of honour led the procession, carrying long burning wax candles, followed by a brilliant train of noble dames and maidens, who had been invited to the ceremony. They were clad in rich stuffs, embroidered in gold and silver, each carrying a large nosegay in one hand and a lemon in the other. The bride was led between George von Hewen and Rheinhardt von Gemmingen, followed by a numerous body of knights and nobles, with Albert von Sturmfeder in the middle, having Maxx Stumpf on his right, and the scribe to the Ulmer council, Dieterich von Kraft, on his left. His whole bearing appeared to be animated by a spirit of elevated joy, his eyes beamed with happiness, and his step was that of a conqueror. His flowing hair, and the waving plumes of his cap, were conspicuously prominent above the heads of those surrounding him. The crowd beheld him as he passed with admiration, the men praising his tall, manly figure and noble gait; and the young girls whispering to each other their remarks upon his fine features and brilliant eyes.

The procession proceeded in this way from the gate of the castle to the church, passing through a broad open space which separated them. The close-packed heads of the worthy citizens of Stuttgardt were all on the stretch to get a sight of the bride and bridegroom as they passed, who, judging by the murmur of applause and admiration which followed them into the church, were flattered by the reception they received.

Among the numerous spectators, a sprightly, plump countrywoman and her daughter seemed particularly anxious to get a sight of the happy. couple. The woman kept curtseying every moment, to the great amusement of the surrounding citizens, who had only paid this attention to the Duke and the bride. She kept up an earnest conversation with her daughter at the same time, who, however, did not appear to heed much what she said. Neither did she seem to be interested in the train of females with their rich dresses, her anxiety being simply to get a glimpse of the bride. As she approached, the young girl's cheeks assumed a deeper red; her red bodice rose and sunk violently, her beating heart appearing likely to break the silver chain with which it was laced. She looked stedfastly at Bertha, and was apparently surprised at the transcendant beauty of the bride, which caused her an involuntary deep sigh. "That's her!" she cried, with peculiar emphasis, hastily concealing her face behind her mother from the gaze of the people about her, who looked astonished at her exclamation.

"Yes, that's her, Barbelle; she is wonderful pretty," whispered the round matron to her daughter, and made a low curtsey; "but now look out for the gentleman."

The girl did not appear to require that piece of advice, for her attention had been long directed to the side whence he was to come. "He comes, he comes!" she heard her neighbours say, "that's him in the white vest and blue mantle, just before the Duke." She saw him; one look only did she dare to cast at him; the blush on her cheek vanished; she trembled, and a tear fell upon her red bodice. When he had passed, she ventured to raise her head again, and look towards him; but it was with an expression of countenance that appeared to indicate more than mere admiration or curiosity.

The procession having by this time entered the church, the spectators crowded to the doors to get in; and in a moment the place which they had occupied was empty. The countrywoman, however, still remained looking at the smart dressed townsfolks, in admiration of their brocade caps, jackets embroidered in gold, and short petticoats. The sight of so much finery awakened in her mind the desire of possessing a dress of the same splendour and shew, only she thought she would not have it cut so low about the neck and shoulders.

Upon turning round, she was startled to see her pretty child concealing her blooming face under her hands. She could not conceive what had happened to the girl; and taking her by both hands, and pulling them down, she observed her weeping most bitterly: "What ails you, Barbelle?" she said, somewhat angrily, but still not without interest, "what makes you cry? did'nt you see him? you ought to be ashamed of yourself! Who ever saw the like? I say, why do you cry?"

"I don't know, mother," she whispered, trying in vain to stop her tears; "I have such a pain in my heart, I don't know why."

"Come, adone with it, I say! or we shall be too late in the church. Hark! how they are playing and singing? Come along, or else I'll not look at you again!" With these words she dragged the girl towards the church. Barbelle followed; and covered her eyes with her white apron, lest the townsfolk should laugh at her. But the deep sighs which she was unable to suppress, made people think she was labouring under some acute suffering. The sounds of the organ and chorus of voices ceased just as they arrived at the entrance of the church. The round matron was aware that the marriage ceremony was now to begin, and therefore endeavoured to push her way through the crowd; but in vain, for as often as she thought to squeeze her plump person into the body of the church, she was sure to be pushed back again with abusive words.

"Come, mother," said the girl, "let's go home. We are poor people, they'll not let us in; come away."

"What? the church is made for every one, poor or rich!" said her mother, indignantly; "make a little room, if you please, we can't see any thing!"

"What?" said the man, whom she addressed, turning to her his well-tanned face, with an immense bushy beard, "what! away with you! we'll not let any one pass. We are his most gracious highness's lansquenet; and our captain has ordered us not to let one soul of you go up to the holy altar. *Morbleu!* I am sorry to swear in the church; but I say, away with you!"

Staberl of Vienna, who was on the spot, interceded for the little girl, but would not consent to her mother entering the church. "Come here, my dear," he called her, "you can see very well here. There; now the priest is putting the ring on her finger, and joins their hands. If you will give me a kiss, I'll get you a better place," and with these words, without waiting for an answer, he stretched out his hand towards Barbelle. She screamed aloud, and ran away, followed by her mother, who vented imprecations on townsfolk in general, and the unmannerly lansquenet.

CHAPTER XXXI

At last I hold thee in my arms,
My best beloved, my own!
Bestowed on me from war's alarms,
Preserved for me alone.

L. Uhland.

Duke Ulerich of Würtemberg was fond of a good table, and when the glass circulated freely in good society, he was not the first to give the signal to break up. At the wedding feast of Bertha von Lichtenstein he remained true to his habits. When the ceremony was finished in the church, the procession returned to the castle much in the same form as it entered, except that the bride and bridegroom walked hand in hand. The company then separated, and wandered about the pleasure-garden of the castle, where they amused themselves among the shrubberies and artificial walks, some looking at the deer and roebucks in the inclosures, others admiring the bears in the dry ditches. At twelve o'clock the trumpets sounded to dinner, which was held in the tournament-hall, a place large enough to entertain many hundred people. This hall was the pride and ornament of Stuttgardt. It was full an hundred paces long; one side of it, looking to the garden, was occupied by numerous large windows, through which the cheerful rays of the sun, piercing the many-coloured glass, illumined this immense apartment, which, by its vaulted roof and numerous pillars, resembled more the interior of a church than a place for festive joy. Galleries extended round the three other sides, hung with rich tapestry, a space being appropriated to the musicians and trumpeters, whilst spectators, assembled to witness the princely feast, occupied the remainder. On other occasions, such as when a tournament took place, these galleries were set apart for the ladies and judges; when, instead of the clang of drinking utensils, the hall resounded with the applauses of the spectators, the heavy blows of swords, the cracking of lances, the whizzing of spears, amidst the laughter and cries of the combatants.

On this day a display of beautiful women and gallant men of all classes had been invited to celebrate the nuptials of the Duke's friend and favourite. They were seated around tables which groaned under loads of good cheer.

The fiddlers in the galleries flourished their fiddlesticks merrily; the cheeks of the trumpeters were swelled to the fullest stretch; the drummers' sticks beat heavily on their skins; and the spectators who were admitted in the other part of the galleries, joined chorus with shouting and hallooing when the company drank a toast. At the upper end of the room sat the Duke upon a throne, under a canopy. His hat was pushed off his forehead, he looked around him with an air of satisfaction, and did not spare the bottle. On his right, at the side of the table, sat Bertha, who was no longer obliged to submit to the ceremonious restraint of cast-down eyes, and keeping at a respectable distance from the bridegroom. Her glance and the expression of her features bespoke happiness. She looked at her husband, who sat opposite to her, and she could scarcely convince herself her being actually a wife was not all a dream, and that the name she had borne eighteen years was changed to that of Sturmfeder. She smiled as often as she regarded him, for it appeared to her that he had already assumed the direction of her conduct. "He is my head," she said to herself, playfully, "my lord, my master!"

And her thoughts were really verified, for Albert felt all the importance and responsibility of his new position in society. It seemed to him as if the young people already paid him more respect than heretofore, and that the old knights treated him more upon an equality since he had become the head of a family, and stood no longer alone in the world. The notions in the good old times were somewhat different to those in the present day respecting the marriage state, for the designation of nobles and citizens was invariably supposed to include that of wife and children, leaving the state of celibacy to monks alone.

The knight of Lichtenstein, Maxx Stumpf von Schweinsberg, and the chancellor, were seated near the Duke, and the scribe to the Council of Ulm was not far from them, being allowed that honour in consequence of his having been the companion of the bridegroom at the wedding. The eyes of the men soon began to sparkle from the effects of the wine, and the cheeks of the ladies to assume a deeper red, when the Duke gave a signal to his headman, and the dinner was removed. The poor people were not forgotten on this occasion; as was always the case on similar rejoicings, the remains of the dinner were taken to the court yard of the castle, and delivered over to them. Pastry and fruit were next brought in, and the wine jugs were replenished by a better sort of the generous liquor for the use of the men, whilst Spanish sweet wine was served to the ladies in small silver cups. This was the moment when, according to the customs of the time, presents were presented to the new-married couple: large baskets were placed beside Bertha to receive them, and when the fiddlers and other musicians had re-tuned their instruments, and began a solemn march, a long brilliant procession moved forward in the hall. Pages of honour led the train, carrying embossed gold tankards and female ornaments of jewelry, as gifts from the Duke to the happy couple.

"May these tankards," said Ulerich, addressing them, "filled with generous liquor, circulate at the marriage feast of your children, and remind you of a man whom both of you served with truth and fidelity in his misfortune, of a Prince who in prosperity forgets not his faithful friends."

Albert was astonished at the value of the presents. "Your Grace's generosity overpowers us," he replied; "love and fidelity claim no reward but the approval of conscience, else they would be too often the price of venality."

"Yes, truly, unless they spring from a source unadulterated by the alloy of all selfish motives, they are but pearls fit only to be thrown to swine," replied the Duke, casting a look of reproof down the length of the table. "We rejoice the more, therefore, to reward your disinterested fidelity, when all seemed to be lost to us. But look, your bride is in tears! I think I know their cause; they are produced by the remembrance of our late painful fate, which I have now recalled to her mind. But away with these tears; they are unpropitious to the day of your wedding. With permission! of your husband," said he, turning to Bertha, "I will now claim payment of an old debt."

Bertha blushed, and cast an anxious look at Albert, fearing the repetition of a liberty which had once highly offended her. He, however, well knew what the Duke meant, for the scene which he had witnessed behind the door was still fresh in his recollection. Amused with the idea of rallying the Duke and his wife upon the subject, he said, "My lord Duke, my wife and I being now one body and one soul, she has my permission to liquidate the debt which I know she owes you."

"Answered as a fine young fellow," returned Ulerich, goodnaturedly; "and I have no doubt that many of our ladies here at table would have no objection to require payment of a similar debt from your handsome mouth; but my demand being addressed solely to the rosy lips of your wife, it refers to her alone."

With these words, he rose and approached Bertha, who looked at her husband in a state of confusion and agitation. "My lord Duke," she said, in a low tone of voice, and holding her head away, "I meant it only in joke--I beseech you!" But Ulerich would not be deterred from his purpose, and wrung his debt with interest from her pretty mouth.

The knight of Lichtenstein during this scene looked angrily, first at the Duke and then at his daughter, fearing his son-in-law might perhaps take umbrage at the liberty, as Ulerich von Hutten had done in a similar case. The chancellor appeared to enjoy a malicious pleasure upon the occasion, at the expense, as he thought, of the young man's feelings. "Hi! hi! hi! I'll empty my glass to your good health," said he to him. "A pretty woman is an excellent petitioner in necessity; I wish you prosperity, dear and most worthy sir;--hi! hi! hi! there is no harm done in the presence of the husband."

"No doubt of it," replied Albert, calmly; "and so much the more innocent because I was present when my wife promised his Grace this proof of her gratitude. The Duke himself proposed to intercede for us with her father to make me his son-in-law, stipulating for this reward on the day of our nuptials."

The Duke started in surprise at these words, and Bertha blushed again, when she thought of the scene which had occasioned the promise. Neither of them, however, contradicted him, deeming it perhaps unseemly, or rather impossible, to charge him with an untruth, or, what was more likely, suspecting they had been overheard.

The Duke could not forbear asking him aside how he came to know the circumstance. Albert acquainted him with it in a few words.

"You are a strange fellow," whispered the Duke, smiling; "what would have been the consequence had I committed the trespass?"

"As I did not know you at that time," replied the other as softly, "I should have run you through on the spot, and hung your body on the nearest oak."

The Duke bit his lips and felt annoyed; but he took his friend's hand, and said, "You would have been perfectly justified, and we should have been justly carried off in our sins. But look, they are bringing more offerings to the bride."

The attendants of the knights and nobles who had been invited to the wedding, appeared, carrying all kinds of curious household utensils, stuffs for wearing apparel, and such like. It being known in Stuttgardt that the feast was given in honour of the Duke's favourite, an embassy of burghers, worthy respectable men, dressed in black, with swords by their sides, short hair and long beards, had been appointed to offer their presents and congratulations upon the occasion. One carried an embossed silver goblet, another a large jug of the same metal ornamented with inlaid medallions and filled with wine. They first approached the Duke in great respect and bowed, and then turned to Albert von Sturmfeder.

The man who bore the goblet, having saluted the bridegroom with a cheerful smile on his countenance, said:

May joy attend the wedded pair,

And bliss increasing be their share!

Accept this gift from Stuttgardt's town,

And length of days your union crown.

'Tis generous wine that cheers the soul,

So come, my comrade, fill the bowl.

The other burgher then filled the goblet with wine from the jug he carried, and whilst his companion drank it out, pronounced:

A cask full stands before your door,

The best of Stuttgardt's wine in store;

And force of body, strength of soul,

Lie deep within the brimful bowl:

Then drain the cup and find them there,

So Stuttgard has obtained her prayer.

Having finished his draught, and replenished the goblet, he repeated the following lines:

Be this your toast when you carouse,

"Long live the Duke and all his house."

Drain to the dregs, then, fill the wine,

"To Sturmfeder and Lichtenstein;"

And may we hope that, as you drink,

You will on Stuttgardt's burghers think.

Albert gave the men both his hands and thanked them for their acceptable presents; Bertha saluted their wives, and the Duke also received them graciously. They laid the silver jug and the goblet in the basket along with the other gifts, retiring respectfully and with solemn step out of the hall. But the burghers were not the only ones to tender their congratulations and manifest their regard for the Duke, in this marked attention to his favourite. Scarcely had they taken their departure, when a disturbance was observed at the door where the lansquenet were on guard, which attracted the notice of the Ulerich. Men's voices were heard swearing and ordering the crowd to obedience to their commands, among which were mingled the voices of women, and one in particular the loudest and most violent was recognized by some of the company at the upper end of the table.

"I declare that is the voice of our Rosel," whispered old Lichtenstein to his son-in-law: "what can her business be about?"

The Duke despatched one of his pages to find out the cause of the noise, and received for answer that some countrywomen were trying to force their way into the hall to present their gifts to the new married couple in spite of the lansquenet, who would not permit them to enter, only because they were common people. Ulerich gave orders immediately to admit them, for, having been pleased with the conduct of the burghers, he promised himself some amusement from the peasants. The attendants having made room for them to pass, Albert, to his astonishment, recognized the wife of the fifer of Hardt, and her pretty daughter, led by her cousin, Mrs. Rosel.

When he was passing from the castle to the church, he thought he recognised the lovely features of the girl of Hardt among the crowd; but more important considerations having engrossed his whole attention, this fleeting apparition was obliterated from his mind. He acquainted the company who the women were, and to whom they belonged. The girl excited great interest, from her being the child of that man whose marvellous actions in the service of the Duke had often been a subject of mystery, and whose fidelity and assistance in time of need contributed essentially to Ulerich's return to his country. The girl had the fair hair, the open forehead, and much the same features of her parent; but the sharp cunning eye, the bold and powerful bearing of the father, were softened into a playful kindliness and natural gaiety which shed a charm around the retiring modesty of his child. As such Albert had known her, when he was in the fifer of Hardt's house, but she now appeared disconcerted before so many persons of rank; it struck him also that her countenance betrayed dejection and sorrow, feelings he had not discovered before on her beautiful features.

Her mother, knowing what good manners were, courtesied all the way up from the entrance door till she arrived at the Duke's chair. The blush of anger still rested upon the wan cheeks of Mrs. Rosel, who felt herself highly aggrieved and insulted by the lansquenet, namely by the Magdeburger and Casper Staberl, who had called her an old withered stick. Before she could compose herself, and present the family of her brother in respectful form to her master, the fifer's wife had already taken the hem of the Duke's mantle and pressed it to her lips. "Good day, my Lord Duke," she said, with deep reverence, "how are you since you have been in Stuttgardt? my husband sends you his compliments. But we don't come to the Duke, no, it is to the knight there," she added, as if recollecting herself, pointing to Albert; "we have brought a wedding present for his wife. There she sits, Barbelle, as large as life."

Mrs. Rosel, confounded at the unceremonious conduct of her sister-in-law before such an august audience, checked her loquacity by saying, "I most humbly beg pardon of your grace, for having brought these people here,--they are the wife and daughter of the fifer of Hardt; pray do not take it ill, your highness, the woman means well, I assure you."

The Duke was more amused with the excuses of Mrs. Rosel than with the blunt language of her sister. "How is your husband?" said he to the countrywoman, "will he visit us soon? why did he not come with you?"

"He has his reasons, sir," she replied; "if war breaks out, he'll certainly not stay at home, for then he may be of some use; but in peaceable times, why he thinks it is not becoming to eat cherries with great folks."

The naïveté of the plump matron almost drove Mrs. Rosel to desperation: she pulled her by the petticoat, and by the long tails of hair, but to no purpose. The wife of the fifer went on talking, to the great amusement of the Duke and his guests, whose irresistible laughter, which her answers elicited, appeared only to increase her happiness and good humour. Barbelle in the meantime, playing with the handle of a little basket she held in her hand, scarcely ventured occasionally to raise her eyes to look at that face which she had beheld with such tender sympathy when she nursed Albert during the long period of his fever. The impression which those days had left on her mind still remained in all its vigour, and the sight of him who had unawares made an inroad into the recesses of her heart, made her fearful of meeting his eye. She heard him say to his wife, "That is the kind girl who nursed me when I lay ill in her father's house, and who conducted me part of the way to Lichtenstein."

Bertha turned to her, and took her hand with great kindness. The girl trembled, and her cheeks assumed a deep blush. She opened her little basket, and presented a piece of beautiful linen, with a few bundles of flax, as fine and soft as silk. She attempted in vain to speak, but kissing the hand of the young bride, a tear fell upon her nuptial ring.

"Eh, Barbelle!" scolded Mrs. Rosel, "don't be so timid and nervous. Gracious young lady,--I would say gracious madame,--have compassion on her; she comes but seldom into the presence of quality folks. There is no one so good who has not two dispositions, says the proverb; the girl can be otherwise as merry and cheerful as larks in spring."

"I thank you, Barbelle," said Bertha: "your linen is very acceptable and very fine. Did you spin it yourself?"

The girl smiled through her tears, and nodded a yes! to speak at that moment appeared to her impossible. The Duke liberated her from this embarrassment only to place her in another still greater. "The fifer of Hardt has truly a very pretty child," he cried, and beckoned to her to approach nearer, "well grown and lovely to behold! only look, chancellor, how well the red bodice and short petticoat become her. Could not we, Ambrosius Bolland, issue an edict for all the beauties in Stuttgardt to adopt this neat dress?"

The chancellor's countenance became distorted into a hideous smile: he examined the blushing maiden from head to foot with his little green eyes; and said, "Certainly, a very good reason could be given, by which an ell might be spared in the length of petticoats, for, as your grace a few years back ordered the weights and measures to be reduced, you have also the right, by all the rules of logic, to shorten the dress of females. But nothing would be gained by it, for--hi! hi! hi! you would see that what was cut off from the bottom, our beauties would be obliged to add above. And who knows whether the ladies would willingly agree to that? They belong to the genus of peacocks, who, you know, don't like to shew their legs."

"You are right, Ambrosius;" the Duke laughed; "nothing escapes a learned man! But tell me, my dear, have you got a sweetheart?"

"Ah! what? your grace!" interrupted the round matron, sharply. "Who would talk about such like things to a child! She is a very good girl, your highness."

The Duke paid no attention to this remark; he enjoyed the embarrassment which was visibly manifest in the chaste features of the innocent girl, who sighed softly, and, playing with the ends of the coloured ribands of her plaited hair, sent an involuntary look to Albert, which seemed to claim his kind offices in her present perplexity, and then suddenly cast her eyes down to the ground. The Duke, alive to every thing that was passing, laughed aloud, in which he was joined by the rest of the men. "Young woman," he said to Bertha, "you may now with justice take part in the jealousy of your husband; if you had seen what I just saw, you might imagine and interpret all kind of things."

Bertha smiled, and, sympathising with Barbelle in her embarrassment, felt how painful the taunts of the men must be to her. Whispering to old Rosel, she told her to take the mother and daughter away. The Duke's sharp eye remarked this also, which his merry mood attributed to jealousy on the part of Bertha. She however unclasped a beautiful cross, set in gold and red stones, which she wore on her neck, attached to a chain, and presenting it to the astonished girl, said, "I thank you with all my heart, my dear Barbelle, for your kindness to my husband; remember me to your father, and come often to us here and in Lichtenstein. What say you, would you like to be in my service? I would endeavour to make you happy, and you would live with your aunt Rosel."

The girl was evidently perplexed at this unexpected proposal. She appeared to combat her feelings, and an assent to it seemed to be struggling through an innocent smile on her countenance, only to be withdrawn again by some other contending feeling. "I thank you very much, gracious lady," she at last uttered, and kissed Bertha's hand, "but I must stay at home; my mother is getting old and wants my assistance. May the Lord, with all his saints, watch over you, and the holy Virgin be gracious to you! May you live in health and be happy with your husband; he is a good, kind gentleman!" Bending down again to kiss Bertha's hand, she then withdrew with her mother and aunt.

"Hearken," called the Duke after them, "if your mother ever consents to give you a husband, bring him to me, and I'll fit you out, my pretty fifer's child!"

By this time it was four o'clock, and the Duke rising from table was the signal for the spectators to quit the galleries, which were immediately furnished with cushions and carpets, and arranged for the reception of the ladies. The tables were removed from the body of the hall, when lances, swords, shields, helmets, and the whole apparatus for tilting were brought in, converting this spacious apartment, which had been but a moment before the scene of festive joy, into a place for the exercise of manly games.

In the present day the education of the fair sex gives them a superior claim to intellectual knowledge and accomplishment over those of the times we narrate. The interest they now take in learned discussion and political argument, and the thirst for novelty which induces many to crowd the rooms of the scientific lecturer, would seem, in some instances, to intrude on the more important duty of domestic employment. Not so was the time of the Swabian matrons and young women occupied. The charge of the house was their sole vocation; but, upon occasions such as the present, their delight was to witness the manly exercise of men, whose bloody strifes were even not unwelcome to their sight. Many a beautiful eye flashed with the noble desire of belonging to a brave combatant. Deep blushes adorned many a cheek, not so much from the fear of seeing her beloved in danger as to witness his retreat from the scene of action, when it was attended with disgrace, or when his arm wielded his sword less powerfully than his antagonist.

Horses were even brought into the hall on this evening, and Bertha had the joy to see her husband obtain a second applause for having made George von Hewen stagger two different times in his saddle. Duke Ulerich von Würtemberg was the bravest combatant of his day, and an ornament to the order of knighthood. History relates of him that, on the day of his own wedding, he overthrew eight of the strongest knights of Swabia and Franconia.

After the tilting had lasted some time, the company adjourned to the hall of the knights for dancing, when the victors of the different games had the precedence in the ball, in all respects similar to the one we have already described. The Duke appeared to have pinned all anxiety and care of the future upon the hump of his chancellor, who sat in a window like a demon of evil destiny, looking upon the surrounding scene with bitter smiles. Raging under an envious feeling of spite, by being debarred from joining in the pleasures of the evening in consequence of the deformity of his person, he remained in his position in sullen silence.

At the end of the last dance Ulerich, the crown of the feast, proposed a parting toast to the young and beautiful bride, but neither he nor Albert could find her in any part of the room. The whisperings and smiles of the ladies betrayed the secret of her having been led away by six of the handsomest maidens, who accompanied her to her dwelling, and, as the custom of those days would have it, to perform the mysterious services of waiting maids.

"Sic transit gloria mundi!" said the Duke, smiling; "but look, Albert, your nuptial companions, with twelve others, are approaching with torches to illumine your path home. But first empty a goblet with us. Cupbearer, go bring us some of our best," he added, addressing the attendants.

Maxx Stumpf von Schweinsberg and Dieterich von Kraft now drew near with torches in their hands, and offered themselves to conduct Albert to his house. Twelve young men followed, each with a torch, to do honour likewise to the bridegroom, for that was also the ceremony used on such occasions. The Duke's cup-bearer brought a full goblet of wine, when having, according to custom, first tasted it himself, he presented it to his master, and then to Albert von Sturmfeder.

Ulerich looked at his friend for a time, evidently moved by a feeling of affection for him. "You have kept your word," said he: "when I was deserted by all the world, dwelling in misery under the earth, you made yourself known to me, when those forty traitors surrendered my castle, and not a spot of Würtemberg was left that I could call my own. You followed me out of the country,--you often consoled me and pointed to this day. Remain, my friend, for who knows what the next day may bring forth. I can now command hundreds who will cry, 'Long live Ulerich!' nevertheless, that shout is far less dear to me than the toast which you gave me in the cavern, and which was re-echoed through its vaults. I'll repeat it, and give it you back again. May you live happy with your wife,--may your offspring blossom and prosper for ever,--and may Würtemberg never fail in hearts as bold in prosperity and faithful in adversity as yours has proved itself!"

The Duke drank, whilst a tear glistened in his eye. The guests cheered and shouted his praise,--the torch-bearers arranged themselves in order,--and Albert von Sturmfeder, led by his two companions, and followed by the rest, was conducted in procession out of the castle to the house of his bride.

CHAPTER XXXII

Hast thou not seen by times the cloudless sky
Sudden illumined by the lightning flash,
And its still, still silence, broken horribly
By the loud music of the thunder crash?
To this we might man's happiness compare,--
To day 'tis present, and to-morrow----where?

Schiller.

The path which the most celebrated novelists of our days generally tread, in their relation of events of ancient and modern times, may be found without the aid of any beacon, and has a direct and fixed limit:--it is the journey of a hero going to a wedding. Let the road be ever so rugged, let him even venture to loiter his time improvidently and inconsistently on his way, he will be induced in the end to hasten his steps so much more rapidly to redeem the lost ground; and so, when an author has at length conducted his reader to the bridal chamber, after having made his hero undergo all the necessary fatigues of his journey with becoming fortitude and resolution, he shuts the door in your face, and closes the book. We might in the same way have ended our story with the gay doings in the castle of Stuttgardt, or included the reader in the torchlight procession of the bridegroom, and conducted him out of our book; but the higher claims of truth and history, together with the interest we have taken in some of the leading characters, compel us to request the reader's patience to accompany us a few steps further, beyond the limit of the bridal-chamber. He will have to bewail with us the destiny of one, who, having begun his career in the midst of misfortune, progressively advanced towards the completion of his best wishes by the energy of his noble mind, until at length his impetuous spirit hurled him again into the depths of misery. His headstrong obstinacy had well nigh involved all his friends in his own sad fate: one alone of them, whose sense of gratitude had indissolubly attached him to the fortunes of his benefactor, preferred rather to risk his life in his service than to desert him in the hour of distress.

Nature's warning voice, which teaches us to be prepared against a reverse of fortune in our happiest days, runs through the world's history.

It is acknowledged by the many, unheeded by the majority, and followed by the few. In all times a troubled spirit has pervaded the habitations of our earth; and, though its influence has been often felt, man has vainly thought to deaden it in the noise of mirth. Ulerich von Würtemberg had heard this warning voice many a night, when he lay on his couch sleepless from a troubled mind. Often times he had started up, thinking he heard the noise of armed men, or the heavy tread of an army approaching nearer and nearer the spot; and, though he convinced himself it was but the night breeze playing through the towers of his castle, a fearful impression still haunted his mind, that his fate was destined to some other awful change. The warnings of his old and tried friend Lichtenstein would often whisper its voice to his mind; in vain he sought to smother it by calling to his aid the artful advice of his chancellor, by which he tried to palliate his own conduct and quiet his conscience. But that faithful monitor upbraided him with having acted without due circumspection and caution since his return to his capital. His enemies, it was well known, had re-assembled a powerful force, with which they threatened the country, and were approaching into the heart of Würtemberg. The imperial town of Esslingen presented itself as a very favourable starting point for their undertakings; being but a short distance from the capital, nearly in the centre of the country: as soon, therefore, as the army of the League could open its communication with it, it became a formidable stronghold, to favour and cover their incursions into Würtemberg. The country people in many places received the Leaguists favourably, for the Duke, by his new regulations, which he had made them swear to, had rendered them distrustful of his intentions. The Würtembergers, from time immemorial, being attached to ancient customs and privileges, handed down through successive generations, regard their old laws and ordinances as so many golden words, though they may scarcely understand their import, or seldom consider whether some reform would not be advantageous.

The peaceable character of the peasant, generally so universal throughout the country, fostered by the tranquil occupations of domestic and agricultural affairs, would lead to a supposition that political strifes were subjects indifferent to their minds; but it was far otherwise: on the occasion of any change or reform in the usages of their ancient laws and customs, which interfered with their ideas of government, they manifested an obstinate caprice, with an ardour and enthusiasm quite out of keeping, and foreign to their ordinary inoffensive dispositions.

The Duke had experienced this love of old institutions in his people, when he some few years back, by the advice of his council, for the purpose of bettering his finances, made an alteration in the public weights and measures. An organised insurrection of peasants, entitled, "The League of Poor Conrad," had made him reflect, and caused the Tübingen compact, which restored the old law, to be introduced. This feeling of attachment to long standing habits was also manifested towards him personally in a very touching manner, when the League entered the country with the intention of expelling the head of the ancient house of their prince. Their fathers and grandfathers having lived under the sway of the Dukes and Counts of Würtemberg, they were filled with dismay and consternation, when a foreign army entered their country to deprive them of their hereditary prince. Their hatred and revenge was excited against the League and their governors; and, though they were compelled by force to submit to their rule, they proved their love to their Lord in many instances of violence towards his enemies.

When their hereditary prince, therefore, a Würtemberger, first returned from exile, the people flocked around him, under the impression that affairs would go on as heretofore. Under his sway they were willing to pay the taxes, to redeem all the state debts, and perform the service done in soccage. There was no murmuring about hard treatment, provided it was done according to ancient usage, and by their legitimate master. But now, the old laws having been expunged by the new oath of fidelity to which they were called upon to swear, the taxes being no longer levied according to old custom, and the whole system being changed, it was no wonder that the people looked upon the Duke as a new master, foreign to their habits, and loudly demanded a return to former rights. They consequently lost all faith in him; not because his hand lay heavier upon them than heretofore; not because he required considerably more from their purses than formerly, but because they regarded the new order of things with a suspicious eye.

A prince, particularly when he lends his ear to such a man as Ambrosius Bolland, seldom learns the true tone of public opinion, and therefore cannot judge whether the measures which his council place before him have been wisely considered. In the present instance, however, the discontent of his people did not escape the penetrating eye of the Duke. He remarked, that he could no more depend upon them, in the event of an extreme difficulty, than he could upon the nobility of the country, who, since his return, had remained neutral spectators of the state of affairs.

He endeavoured to screen from public notice the uneasiness which these observations caused him; and for this purpose he assumed an extravagant tone of gaiety, which often succeeded to blind himself, and make him forget the precipice upon which he stood: and for the sake of instilling confidence into the people, and into the army which he had assembled in and about Stuttgardt, he determined to revenge himself with double interest upon the League, for the depredations they had committed in excursions from Esslingen. He beat and repulsed them indeed, and wasted their territory; but when he returned in victory from his expedition, he could not conceal from himself, that, considering his own slender resources, the fortune of war might go against him, when once the army of his enemies should be brought into the field. His apprehensions were soon verified; for the rapid advance of the League's troops towards the capital threatened the stability of Ulerich's present doubtful position. Upon the turn of a battle, which now seemed inevitable, depended his very existence.

Little or nothing was known in Stuttgardt of a summons which had been sent to the Duke from the League. The court lived in its usual round of gaiety; tranquillity and joy reigned in the town; when all of a sudden, on the 12th, of October, the lansquenets which the Duke had encamped near Cannstadt, a short distance from the capital, came into the town in confusion, with the intelligence that they had been driven in by a large force of the League. The inhabitants of Stuttgardt were now convinced that an important crisis was at hand; they conjectured that the Duke must long since have been aware of this threatening attack, for he immediately assembled his officers, drew in his troops, which were scattered about in quarters in the villages surrounding the capital, passed his army in review, amounting to upwards of ten thousand men, on the same evening; and in the night marched with a large body of infantry, to reinforce the posts which a division of the lansquenet still occupied between Esslingen and Cannstadt.

The departure of all the men, young and old, who could carry arms, caused many a beautiful eye to weep that night, when they marched out of Stuttgardt with the Duke, to the field of battle; but the wailing of the women and young maidens was drowned in the warlike noise of the marching army, resembling the sobs of a child amidst the raging of the elements. Bertha's grief, though almost overpowering, was silent, as she accompanied her husband to the door, where his servants awaited him and her father with their horses. They had enjoyed the first days of their marriage alone and in quiet, mutually engaged in the affectionate offices of each other's happiness. Dreaming little of the future, they thought themselves safe in the haven of uninterrupted love; and whilst they lived but for themselves, the whisperings, the mysterious disquietude which agitated the public mind, were unheeded by them. Having been long accustomed to see the knight of Lichtenstein serious and thoughtful, they did not attribute the alteration which his features had of late assumed, to any cause beyond the natural anxiety he was known to feel in the present state of the Duke's affairs. Neither did they, for the same reason, apprehend any immediate disaster to disturb their happiness, although they remarked a certain air of fearful anticipation and despair which at times clouded his brow. The old man witnessed the happiness of his children, and participated in it; and, not wishing to interrupt their bliss unnecessarily, he concealed from them his uneasiness upon the state of affairs; but at length the threatening crisis approached. The Duke of Bavaria had advanced into the heart of the country, and the call to arms startled Albert out of the embrace of his beloved wife.

Nature had gifted her with a strength of mind, and a superiority of character, which entered into every transaction of her life, and exists only in that purity of soul which commits its dearest interests into the hands of a higher Power, with implicit confidence. Aware of what was due to the honour of her husband's name, and the relationship in which he stood to the Duke, she repressed her grief, and the only sacrifice which the infirmity of her nature offered for the many dangers to which her beloved husband would necessarily be exposed, was an involuntary flood of tears.

"I cannot believe, dearest Albert, that we are never to see each other again!" she said, whilst a forced smile illumined her beautiful face: "we have but just begun to live; heaven will not cut us off in the bud of a happy existence; I can, therefore, part from you in tranquillity, in the conviction that you will soon be restored to me."

Albert kissed her soft weeping eye, which dwelt upon him so full of tenderness, and whose glance inspired him with consolation and fortitude. In this distressing moment he thought not of the danger he was going to encounter, his only concern was the consideration of the affliction of the beloved being he held in his arms, should he be left on the field of battle. The mere thought of the painful existence she would then lead in solitude, and in the remembrance of the few days of their bliss, unmanned him. He pressed her in his arms, as if to drive away these agonizing ideas from his mind; he gazed with intense love upon her endearing eye, seeking to obliterate the heart-rending feelings of the moment; but his heart, though rent by the afflicting struggle of separation, was inspired with hope and confidence. He at length forced himself from her embrace.

The two knights joined the Duke at the gate leading to Cannstadt. The night was dark, only enlivened by the dim light of the first quarter of the moon and the host of stars. Albert observed the Duke to look gloomy, and wrapped in deep thought. His eyes were cast down, as if to avoid observation, and he rode on in profound silence, after he had saluted them hastily with his hand.

There is something peculiarly solemn and striking in the night march of an army. By day, the sun, a cheerful country, the sight of many comrades, the change of scenery, invite the soldier to beguile time by conversation and the merry song; and, because outward impressions forcibly engage the attention, little is thought among them of the object of the march, of the uncertainty of war, or of futurity, which is veiled to no one more than to the military man. Very different is a march by night. The hollow sound of the tread of the troops, the regular pacing of horses, their snorting, the clatter of arms, only break the stillness of night, whilst the mind, no longer able to dwell on surrounding objects, impressed by these monotonous sounds, becomes thoughtful and serious; joking and laughter cease to cheer the march, loud talk sinks into whispering, and thought, no longer occupied with indifferent subjects, is taken up with speculations upon what is likely to be the result of the campaign.

Such was the complexion of the march of that night, gloomy, and uninterrupted by any shout of animating joy. Albert rode by the side of the old knight of Lichtenstein, occasionly casting an anxious look at him, for he sat in his saddle as if bent down by grief, with an expression of thoughtfulness on his countenance, more strongly marked than he had ever noticed before. Animation seemed almost suspended, and nothing gave indication of life in him, but an occasionally deep-drawn sigh, or when his keen eye was raised in contemplation of the pale moon.

"Do you think we shall have a skirmish tomorrow?" whispered Albert to him, after a time.

"Skirmish!--we shall have a battle," was the short answer.

"How! do you really believe that the army of the League is strong enough now to attempt to stand its ground against us? It's impossible! Duke William must have possessed wings to have brought up his Bavarians so soon, and we know that Fronsberg is still undecided as to his intentions. I don't believe they have many more than six thousand men."

"Twenty thousand," answered the old knight, in an under tone of voice.

"By heavens! I had no idea of that," replied the young man in astonishment. "We shall certainly have hard work, if that be the case; but we have well trained and experienced troops, and the League's army cannot boast of an eagle eye compared to the Duke's, not even excepting Fronsberg's. With such an advantage on our side, do you not think the chances are in our favour?"

"No," was the answer of the old man.

"Well, I'll not give up all hope. We have also a still greater advantage in our cause: we fight for our country, whereas the views of the League are mercenary. That circumstance alone will inspire our troops with courage. The Würtembergs will defend their father-land."

"That is just what I least depend upon," answered Lichtenstein. "Had not the Duke been obstinate in forcing the country to swear to the new oath of allegiance, the case would be far different, he would have had the hearts of the people with him; but now, force alone compels them to fight under his banners. The result is dubious."

"I admit what you say to be true, and that the Duke has lost much by the imprudence of his measures," replied Albert; "but I have great faith in the honest patriotism of the Swabians, and, in spite of everything he has done, they will not desert their hereditary Prince in the hour of need, and in the defence of his lawful rights. Where do you think we shall meet the enemy? Where shall we take up a position?"

"The lansquenets have thrown up a few redoubts at Untertürkheim, between Esslingen and Cannstadt, and have three thousand five hundred men there; we shall join them tonight."

The old man was silent, and they rode on for some time side by side, without speaking.

"Hearken, Albert!" he began again; "I have often looked death in the face, and am old enough not to fear to stand in such a predicament again. We are all liable to the common lot of mortals. If anything happens to me, console my dear child, Bertha!"

"Father!" cried Albert, grasping his hand, "pray do not think of such things; you will still live long and happy with us!"

"Perhaps so," replied the old man, with a firm voice, "perhaps not. It were folly in me to beg of you not to risk yourself too much in the battle; you would not follow my advice; but I pray you to think of your young wife, and do not rush into danger blindly, and without good reason. Promise me this."

"I promise! here is my hand; where duty calls me, I cannot shrink from it; unnecessarily I'll not expose myself; but you, also, my dear father, must give me the same promise."

"We'll not talk about that at present. If I, by chance, am called out of this life to-morrow, my last will, which I have placed in the Duke's hands, will be fulfilled. Lichtenstein will pass into your possession, and you will be invested with the property. My name will die with me in the country; may yours live in its remembrance so much the longer!"

The young man was overcome at these last words of his high-minded, venerable father: he endeavoured to answer him, but the rush of painful thoughts to his mind prevented all utterance. A known voice at the moment called him by name. It was the Duke's. He pressed the hand of his wife's parent, and rode in haste to Ulerich.

"Good morning, Sturmfeder!" said the Duke, who appeared more cheerful; "I say good morning, for I hear the cock crow in the village. How did you leave your wife? was she very much overcome when you last saw her?"

"She wept," answered Albert; "but she uttered not a word of complaint."

"Just like her, by Saint Hubertus! we have seldom seen so much fortitude in a woman. If the night were not quite so dark, I would like to see in your eye whether your heart is tuned to the battle, and if you are inclined to close with the Leaguists?"

"Show me but the path I am to follow, and you'll not find me swerve from it, though it lead into the thickest of the battle. Does your grace imagine, that, during the few days of my marriage, I have so totally forgotten the lesson I learnt of you, namely, never to lose courage in prosperity or adversity?"

"You are right--impavidum ferient ruinæ; we expected nothing less from our faithful banner-bearer; but another must perform that office to-day. I have selected you for a more important service. You will take these hundred and sixty cavalry by our side, choose one of them to show you the way, and trot on direct to Untertürkheim. It is possible the road may not be open, as the Leaguists from Esslingen may have come down to dispute the passage with us. How would you act under such circumstances?"

"I would throw myself with my hundred and sixty horsemen among them, and cut my way through; that is to say, if their whole force were not in the neighbourhood. If I found them too strong, I would cover my position, until you came up with reinforcements."

"You have well said, spoken like a valiant swordsman, and if you deal your blows as heavily on them as you did on me at Lichtenstein, you'll cut through six hundred Leaguists. The people I have given you are staunch. They are composed of the butchers, saddlers, and blacksmiths of Stuttgardt and the surrounding towns. I know them in many a hard fight. Brave, and able to sever the skull down to the breast bone, they will follow you, sword in hand, wherever you may lead them, when once they are well inclined towards you; let them have but one good blow at the brain, no doctor's hand need attempt a cure. That's the right sort of Swabian cut."

"Am I to take post at Unterützkheim?"

"You will find there the lansquenet under George von Hewen and Schweinsberg encamped on a hill. The watchword is, 'Ulerich for ever!' Tell them they must keep the position till five o'clock; before day-break I shall be with them with six thousand men, and then will await the Leaguists. Farewell, Albert!"

The young man returned the salute by bowing respectfully, and putting himself at the head of the gallant band, trotted down the valley with them. The men were powerful figures, broad shouldered and well limbed, whose animated fearless looks beheld their young leader with satisfaction, as he placed himself in their front, and appeared honoured by his command. Having run his eye rapidly through the ranks, he selected one whose penetrating eye and intelligent countenance seemed to point him out as the fittest person to act the part of guide. He immediately called him to his side, and gave him the necessary directions. They approached the foot of the Rothenberg, on the summit of which stood the hereditary castle of the house of Würtemberg, commanding an extended view over the valley of the Neckar. It was but faintly illumined by the glimmer of the stars, and Albert could not distinctly distinguish its form, though he kept his eyes fixed upon its towers and walls. He recollected that night in the cavern, when the Duke spoke in sorrow of the castle of his ancestors, and described the country seen from its towers as abounding in corn, wine, and fruit, all of which he once could call his own. The young man sank into reflection upon the unhappy fate of the Duke, which now again appeared to contend with him for the possession of his patrimony. He dwelt upon the extraordinary mixture in his character, the foundation of which was truly great, but was too often disturbed by rage, malice, and unbending pride. "If you look between those two trees, you will be able to distinguish the points of the towers of Untertürkheim," said the man, who was conducting him on the road. "The road is much more level now, and if we push on, we shall soon be there."

Albert spurred his horse, and the rest following his example, soon gained sight of the village. A double line of lansquenet was stationed outside of it, who at their approach presented their halberds in fearful array, whilst the red glimmer of burning matches was seen scattered about in many points, like the glow-worm sparkling in the night.

"Who comes there?" cried a deep voice from the ranks: "Give the watch-word!"

"Ulericus for ever," answered Albert von Sturmfeder: "who are you?"

"Good friends!" answered Maxx Stumpf Schweinsberg, stepping out of the ranks of the lansquenet, and riding towards the young man. "Good morning, Albert; you have kept us waiting somewhat long. We have been all night upon our legs, anxiously expecting a reinforcement, for in the wood there over against us it does not look pleasant, and if Fronsberg had been aware of his advantage, he might have overpowered us long ago."

"The Duke is coming up with six thousand men," replied Sturmfeder, "and will be here in two hours at furthest."

"Six thousand only, did you say? by Saint Nepomuk, that's not enough! we have but three thousand five hundred here, so that all we can muster in the field will make little more than nine thousand. Are you aware that the Leaguists are over twenty thousand strong? What artillery does the Duke bring with him?"

"I don't know--it was only just arrived when we departed," replied Albert.

"Well, come, and let the men dismount, and take some rest," said Maxx Stumpf; "they'll have work enough this day."

The cavalry dismounted, and laid down to rest. The lansquenet also were permitted to fall out of their ranks, leaving strong piquets on the heights, and on the Neckar. Maxx Stumpf gave all the necessary directions for the remainder of the night; and Albert von Sturmfeder, rolling himself in his cloak, also laid down to repose himself from the fatigues of the past twenty-four hours, and refresh himself for the coming strife. The stillness of the morning, broken only by the monotonous tone of the sentry's call, soon lulled him to sleep, with the last thought directed in prayer to God, into whose hands he resigned himself and his beloved wife.

CHAPTER XXXIII

Enveloped in the smoke,

Both man and horse are hidden;

Away they now have broke,

Now down the hill have ridden:

Across the Neckar springs the steed so good,

And in the valley is the fight renew'd.

G. Schwab.

Albert was roused a little before break of day by the roll of drums, calling the little band to arms. A small border of light was visible on the horizon, the advanced guard of day, when the troops of the Duke were seen coming up in the distance. The young man put on his helmet and armour, mounted his horse, and, at the head of his men, waited to receive the Duke. The stern features of Ulerich had lost none of their thoughtful expression, though all traces of gloom had disappeared from them. From his eyes beamed a warlike fire, and his countenance bespoke courage and determination. Clad entirely in steel, he wore a green cloak, trimmed with gold, over his heavy armour, whilst the colours of his house waved in the large floating plumes of his helmet. The rest of his dress differed in nothing from that of the knights and nobles about him, who, all clad in polished steel, "up to the eyes," formed a circle around the Duke. They saluted Hewen, Schweinsberg, and Sturmfeder in a friendly way, and made inquiries about the position of the enemy.

Nothing was as yet to be seen of the troops of the League, except on the border of the wood towards Esslingen, where a few straggling out-posts were observed to be stationed. The Duke determined to quit the height which the lansquenet occupied, and take up a position in the plain beneath. His army being much inferior in cavalry to the League, who, according to the reports of spies, could muster three thousand horses, he hoped the flanks of this position, having the Neckar on one side and a thick wood on the other, which he intended to take up in the valley, would make up for the deficiency in numbers.

Though the opinion of Lichtenstein, with many others, was against this plan, fearing the army would be exposed to the fire of artillery from the surrounding heights, Ulerich would not be dissuaded from it, and ordered the army to march accordingly. Having arranged his order of battle close to the town of Türkheim, he there awaited his enemy. Albert von Sturmfeder was directed to remain near him with the cavalry, which had been entrusted to his command, to be ready to strike a decisive blow, and at the same time to form his body guard; whilst Lichtenstein, with four-and-twenty other knights, joined themselves to this mounted body of burghers, ready to support them in the event of an attack of cavalry. In those days a battle was often an affair of so many single-handed combats. The knights who followed an army seldom fought in solid masses; but with a quick eye, they marked out an adversary from among the ranks of the enemy, rode at him, and fought him with lance and sword. Such a band of gallant men, headed by old Lichtenstein, was that which now closed with Albert's troop. The Duke himself, burning with the desire of wielding his powerful arm, and proving the renown of his far-famed prowess in single combat, was only controlled in this romantic idea by the pressing exhortations of his friends. A most extraordinary figure was seen to keep his station by the side of the Duke, in appearance more like a tortoise on horseback, than a human being. A helmet, with a large feather, protruded high above a small body, upon the back of which sat an arched coat of mail. The little horseman's knees were bent high up on the saddle, whilst his hand kept a fast hold of the pummel. The closed vizor of the unknown knight concealed his face from Albert's observation; who, curious to ascertain who the ridiculous looking warrior might be, rode up to the Duke to satisfy himself, and said:

"Upon my word, your highness has provided yourself with a marvellous looking animal as a guide. Only observe his withered legs, his trembling arm, the enormous helmet between his shoulders;--who may this pigmy be?"

"Don't you recognize the hump?" asked the Duke, laughing. "Just observe the extraordinary coat of mail he has on; it is for all the world like a large nutshell, to protect his back, in case he has to run for it. He is my faithful chancellor, Ambrosius Bolland."

"By the holy Virgin! what an unjust opinion I have formed of him," replied Albert; "I never thought he would have drawn a sword or mounted a horse, and there he sits upon a beast as big as an elephant, and carries a sword as long as himself. I never should have given him credit for so martial a spirit."

"Do you suppose it is his own free-will which impels him to attend me in the field? No, I have been obliged by force to make him follow me. Having pushed me to extremities against my will, in order to satisfy his wicked intentions, which I fear has placed me upon the brink of a precipice, he shall partake of the soup himself which he has cooked for me. He wept when I insisted on his coming with me; complaining of his gout, and other infirmities, saying his nature was not military; but I made him buckle on his armour, and put him on a horse, the most fiery beast in my stable. He shall have the bitters as well as the sweets of his counsel."

During this discourse the knight of the hump threw open his vizor, and discovered his pale affrighted countenance. The eternal hypocritical smile had vanished, his piercing little eyes had swollen beyond their ordinary size, and assumed a staring look, turning slowly and timidly from side to side; a cold perspiration sat upon his forehead, and his voice had softened down into a trembling whisper. "For the mercy of God, most worthy Albert von Sturmfeder, most beloved friend and benefactor," said he, "pray say a good word for me to our obdurate master, that he may release me from this masquerading gambol. The ride in this heavy armour has most cruelly tormented me, the helmet presses on my brain, setting all my thoughts on the dance, and my knees are bent with the gout. Pray, pray do! say a kind word for your humble servant, Ambrosius Bolland; I will certainly repay it ten-fold."

The young man turned away in disgust, from the cowardly sinner. "My Lord Duke," said he, whilst a blush of high-minded scorn and contempt coloured his cheeks, "permit him to go. The knights have drawn their swords, and pressed their helmets firmer on their foreheads; the people shake their spears, impatient for the signal of attack; why, then, should a coward be counted among the ranks of men?"

"He remains, I say," replied the Duke, with a stern voice; "the first step he makes to the rear, I'll cut him down from his horse. The devil sat upon your blue lips, Ambrosius Bolland, when you advised us to despise our people, and subvert the laws of the land. This day, when the balls whiz and swords clatter, shall you know whether your counsel has proved of advantage to us or not."

The chancellor's eyes beamed with rage, his lips trembled, and his whole countenance was fearfully distorted. "I only gave you my advice,--why did you follow it?" said he; "you are the Duke and master; you gave the orders for swearing the oath of allegiance,--how could I help it?"

The Duke, in anger at these words, turned his horse with such velocity towards him, that the chancellor, expecting his last moment was come, bent himself down in trepidation on his horse's mane. "By our princely honour," he cried, with a terrible voice, his eyes flashing fire, "we are astonished at our own forbearance. You took advantage of the blindness of our anger, when first we re-entered our capital; you knew too well how to ingratiate yourself into our confidence. Had we not followed your counsel, thou serpent, we should have had twenty thousand Würtemberg hearts as a wall to defend their Prince. Oh! my Würtemberg! my Würtemberg! Had I but followed the advice of my old friend! There is indeed a charm in the love of my people!"

"Away with these thoughts," said the old knight of Lichtenstein. "We are on the eve of battle; all is not yet lost; we have still time to repair the wrongs we have committed. You are surrounded by six thousand Würtembergers, and, by heavens! they will be victorious, if you lead them with confidence to the enemy. We are all friends here, my Lord! forgive your enemies; dismiss your chancellor, who can be of no service to you, he cannot use a sword."

"No! remain by my side, thou tortoise! dog of a scribe!" said the Duke. "Seated in your office, you wrote laws with your own hand, and despised my people, you shall now witness how they can fight; how a Würtemberger can conquer or----die. Ha! do you see them on the height there? do you see the flag with the red cross? there's the banner of Bavaria; how their arms glisten in the dawn of the morning, and their helmet plumes wave in the breeze! Good morning, gentlemen of the Swabian League; that is a sight for a Würtemberger! how my heart gladdens at it!"

"Look! they are preparing their artillery," interrupted Lichtenstein; "you must not remain on this spot, my Lord, your life is in danger; go back, go back; send us your orders from yonder tree, (pointing to one at a distance,) where you will be in safety; this position belongs to us alone."

The Duke turned to him, and answered, with an air of proud dignity, "Where did you ever hear that a Würtemberger retreated when the enemy had sounded the attack? My ancestors never knew what fear was, and their posterity shall also, like them, never betray the motto, 'Fearless and true!' Observe how the brow of the mountain becomes darker and darker with their numerous bodies of men. Do you see that white cloud on yonder hill, tortoise? do you hear it crack? that's the thunder of artillery, that pours into our ranks. If you have a clear conscience at this moment, make up your accounts with this world; for no one would give a penny for your life."

"Let us say a prayer," said Maxx von Schweinsberg, "and then at them, in God's name."

The Duke piously raised his hands and eyes towards heaven, and his companions following his example, they said their prayers, imploring the aid of the Almighty in the justice of their cause. This was the general custom of the good old times, before the battle commenced. The thunder of the enemy's artillery contrasted terribly with the deep silence which reigned about this group, now engaged in soliciting God's protection. Each appeared deeply impressed with the solemnity of the few moments which were perhaps left to them in this world, except the chancellor Ambrosius Bolland, who clasped his hands, whilst his eyes were not directed in faith to heaven, but wandered to the enemy's heights. His trembling body, as he observed the fire and smoke of each gun from the League, proved that his soul was not leaning upon Him who makes his sun to shine upon the good and upon the evil.

When Ulerich von Würtemberg and those around him had finished their solemn duty, he drew his sword, which was immediately followed by the rest, and in a moment a thousand blades glittered in the sun. "The lansquenet are already engaged," said he, casting his eagle eye rapidly down the valley. He now issued his orders with a cool determined voice, and, addressing George von Hewen, directed him to support them with a thousand infantry. Turning then to Schweinsberg, he said, "Take eight hundred men to the skirt of the wood, and remain there till further directions. Reinhart von Gemmingen, march with your division, and take position in the middle space between the wood and the Neckar. And you, Albert von Sturmfeder, remain here with your brigade of cavalry, and be ready to advance at a moment's notice. And now may God be with you all, my friends! Should we be destined not to see each other again in this world, we shall meet the sooner in the next." He saluted them by lowering his immense sword. The knights returned it, and advanced with their respective bodies of men towards the enemy, rending the air with loud vivas of "Ulerich for ever!"

The army of the League having taken up the ground which the Duke's men had shortly before occupied, saluted their enemy from the mouths of several pieces of heavy ordnance, moving slowly down into the valley, with the apparent intention of crushing them by superior numbers. At the moment when their last division had quitted this position, the Duke turned to Albert von Sturmfeder, and said, "Do you see those guns on the height?"

"Yes, and they are supported by a very few men apparently," he answered.

"Fronsberg supposes that because we cannot fly over to him, it would be impossible to take his pieces. But there is a path in the wood there," said the Duke, pointing with his hand, "which leads to the left, into a field, which field skirts the hill. If you advance cautiously with your cavalry, and follow the path, you will get almost into the rear of the enemy. And if you succeed, pull up your horses a moment to give them wind, and then gallop up the hill, and their artillery is ours."

Albert bowed to him at parting, whilst the Duke gave him his hand. "Farewell, young man," said he; "it grieves us to send so young a married man upon such dangerous service; but we know of none other better calculated or more determined than yourself to perform it."

The cheeks of the young hero glowed with ardour when he heard these words, and his eyes bespoke confidence in the bold enterprise he was about to undertake. "I thank you, my lord, for this new proof of your consideration," he replied; "you do me a greater kindness than if you had endowed me with one of your most valuable estates. Farewell, father," turning to old Lichtenstein, "remember me to my beloved wife."

"I don't mean to let you go alone," replied the old knight, smiling: "I'll accompany you. Under your conduct----"

"No, remain with me, old friend," entreated the Duke; "do you wish me to follow the chancellor's counsel in the field also? He might lead me into a much worse scrape than he has already done. Stay by my side, old man; make a hasty farewell with your son, for there is not a moment to lose."

The old knight pressed the hand of the young man, who returned it smiling, and, in a cheerful mood, placed himself at the head of his gallant band, when he galloped away with the Stuttgardt burghers, leading them towards the enemy in this critical moment, crying, "Ulerich for ever!" Having reached the skirt of the wood, he had a moment's leisure to run his eye over the field of battle. The Würtembergers were in very good position, their flanks being covered by the wood and the Neckar, and their centre arranged in such a manner as to be able to repel any serious charge of cavalry. It was therefore evident, that any alteration in their present line of battle would subject them to extreme danger. The great disadvantage under which they laboured was the fact of their being inferior to their enemy by two-thirds of the number of combatants and though the Leaguists were unable to bring their whole force into action at once, in consequence of the confined space of the valley, their superiority of numbers compensated for the want of room to manœuvre in, which consideration alone required the most strenuous exertions of Ulerich's small band to maintain their ground. They, indeed, with such fearful odds against them, kept their line unbroken, and their courage appeared to rise still higher as their ranks began to thin. But, though the brave Swabians valiantly disputed every inch of ground, it was to be apprehended lest, by dint of renewed attacks by fresh troops, they would ultimately be forced to give way.

These fleeting observations which Albert had been enabled to make, convinced him that upon some daring piece of service depended the success of the day. The energies of his mind rose in proportion to the difficulties he had to contend with. He felt that Ulerich's destiny was now in his keeping, and that one bold stroke, such as he was about to undertake, would decide the fate of the contest.

His troop having now reached the wood, they proceeded through it in silence and with caution, aware of the advantage which infantry possess over cavalry under such circumstances. But they arrived at the point leading to the field which the Duke had described, without molestation. To the right beyond the wood the battle raged in full fury. The cheers of the attacking part, the roar of artillery and small arms, the noise of the drums, echoed terribly through its trees.

The hill lay before them, from the summit of which several pieces of heavy artillery played upon the ranks of the Würtembergers. The path to the top of it, leading up from the side of the wood, being of gentle ascent, Albert was astonished at the quick eye of the Duke in having discovered the only weak part of the enemy's position, every other point of it being unassailable, at least by cavalry. The guns, as far as he could observe from the place where he stood, were not supported by any considerable force, and, therefore, as soon as the horses had rested a few moments, Albert sounded the charge, and, putting himself at their head, galloped up the hill in gallant style, and reached the summit in an instant, calling to the enemy to surrender. The consternation of the Leaguist troops in thus finding their enemies suddenly among them, paralysed all their means of defence; whilst the brave butchers, saddlers, and blacksmiths of Stuttgardt, taking advantage of their confusion, dealt out the true Swabian cut on the heads of their adversaries, and in a short time reduced the covering party to a small number. Albert threw a triumphant look down the plain towards the Duke; he heard the exulting shouts wafted to him from the throats of many thousand Würtembergers, and saw them advance with renewed courage, being now relieved from the galling fire of the artillery on the hill.

He was obliged, however, to check this momentary joy of victory, in consideration of his retreat, the second and most difficult operation of the gallant undertaking; for the Leaguists, having observed the sudden cessation of their artillery, had ordered a powerful body of cavalry to charge the hill. As there was no time to bring away the captured guns, he quickly ordered his men to fill them with stones and earth, rendering them by this means unserviceable, and then casting his eye towards the line of retreat, he perceived he would have to contend with difficulties he had not anticipated.

To retrace the path through the wood by which, he had advanced was his first thought, for, were it even occupied by the enemy's cavalry, he would meet them upon equal terms. But, to his dismay, as he was about to put it into execution, he observed that a large body of the Leaguist infantry had already gained the wood to cut off his passage through it, rendering it thereby impossible for him to join his comrades by that road. To attempt to cut through the enemy's army with only one hundred and sixty horsemen, would seem to be absolute madness. The only alternative left to him, therefore,--and it was one more likely to lead to death than deliverance,--was to make direct for the Neckar, which flowed between him and his friends, and pass it by swimming across. Desperate as this only resource of escape was, he determined to act upon it without loss of time, and once having gained the banks of the river, he thought the passage of it might be easily accomplished. By these means he might hope to join the Duke; though it was but a forlorn hope. Five hundred men of the Leaguist cavalry had by this time reached the foot of the hill upon which he stood. He thought he recognized Truchses von Waldburg at their head, and rather than surrender to him, he would willingly have suffered death.

He gave the signal to his gallant Würtembergers to follow him down the side of the hill which led to the banks of the river. They staggered at the fearful expedient, for it was scarcely to be expected that a fifth part of them would escape, so steep was the descent, and besides which, between the hill and the river stood a large body of the enemy's infantry, ready to receive them. But their gallant young leader, throwing open his vizor, discovered to them his noble countenance, beaming with the inspiration of heroic magnanimity. The whole troop were animated by the same bold spirit, and when they recollected they had seen him but a few weeks back leading a beautiful maiden to the altar, and that he had left this endearing object behind him, for the sake of his Duke and country, they vociferated in loud shouts the practices of their several vocations. "At them!" cried the butchers, "we'll slaughter them like oxen;" "And we'll hammer them like hot iron," cried the blacksmiths; and the saddlers vociferated "They shall be beat as soft as leather." "Ulerich for ever!" cried their bold-hearted leader, who putting spurs to his horse, was the first to gallop down the dangerous declivity. The enemy's cavalry could scarcely believe their eyes when they arrived at the top of the hill, in expectation of capturing their daring adversaries, and saw them hotly engaged with their infantry at the bottom of it. This bold step of Albert's cost many a brave man his life: many were thrown from their horses, and fell into the hands of the Leaguists; but the major part, arriving safely at the foot of the hill, were engaged hand to hand with the enemy, and the helmet plumes of their leader were seen to wave high in the midst of the fray. The ranks of the infantry were soon broken by the impetuous charge of the Würtembergers, who now pushed for the bank of the Neckar, and following their leader, dashed into the water to cross it. Though his horse was a powerful beast he had not strength sufficient to bear the weight of his rider, clad in armour, nor to stem its stream, at present swollen beyond its ordinary height by heavy rains. He was on the point of sinking, calling to his men not to think of him, but to push on to the Duke, and give him his last farewell, when at this critical moment two gallant blacksmiths, having disencumbered themselves of their horses, seized the young knight, one by his arms, and the other taking his horse's bridle, landed him in safety on the opposite bank.

The Leaguists sent many a shot after their flying enemy, but fortunately they fell harmless. In the sight of both armies, this daring band continued its further route unmolested to the Duke. Having passed a deep ford, not far from the spot where Ulerich was stationed, they were received with loud shouts of joy and applause by their companions.

Though a considerable part of the enemy's artillery had been rendered unserviceable by the no less bold than rapid attack of Albert von Sturmfeder, such was the unhappy fate of Duke Ulerich, that even this brilliant feat of arms could not avert the spell which seemed to hang over his destiny. The strength of his people began to fail under renewed attacks of superior numbers. In spite of the experience and bravery of the lansquenets, who gave proofs of the honesty of their promises to the Duke, and though they continued to uphold their accustomed warlike character, and did not cede an inch of ground, the loss they had sustained obliged their commanders to form them into circles to repel the charges of cavalry. The line of battle being thereby broken, the vacant spaces were but feebly filled up and sustained by the country people, badly armed, and worse soldiers, having been brought into the field in haste, and almost without discipline. At this critical moment intelligence arrived of the Duke of Bavaria having suddenly surprised and taken possession of Stuttgardt, that a fresh army was coming up in the rear, and was scarcely a quarter of an hour's distance off. This news was a death-blow to the Duke's hopes, who now perceived there was nothing left to him but flight or death to prevent his falling into the hands of his enemies. What was to be done in this emergency? His followers advised him to throw himself into the hereditary castle of the house of Würtemberg, and there remain until he could find an opportunity secretly to escape. He turned his eyes towards the place, his last resource, which, lighted up by the brilliancy of the day, seemed to look down in stern majesty upon the valley, where the descendant of him who raised it had staked his last hope in one desperate conflict. But when he saw the red flag playing in the morning breeze over the towers and walls of his castle, he turned pale, and pointing to it, was unable to give utterance to the painful feelings which the sight occasioned. The knights directing their attention to it, discovered a black smoke issuing from all corners, a proof that the victorious flag had been planted on its pinnacle amidst the flames lighted up by an avenging enemy. Würtemberg now burnt at every point, and her unhappy master witnessed the spectacle in ghastly despair. Both armies also noticed the burning castle. The Leaguists saluted the event with loud shouts of exulting joy, whilst the courage of the Würtembergers sank in proportion, and viewed the sad sight as the setting sun of the Duke's prosperity.

The drums of the army advancing in the rear were now heard distinctly approaching towards them; the armed peasantry, in many places, began to give way, when Ulerich said, in a firm, voice, addressing those immediately about him, "Whoever means honourably by us, follow me, we'll cut our way through their hosts, or fall in the attempt. Take my banner in your hand, valiant Sturmfeder, and charge their ranks with us." Albert seized the flag of Würtemberg, the Duke placed himself by his side, the knights and burghers on horseback surrounded them, and prepared to open a passage for their lord. The Duke pointed to a weak position in the enemy's line, which appeared the one most favourable to ensure the success of the daring project; if the attempt failed, all was lost. Albert volunteered for the desperate post of honour of leading the determined band; but the old knight of Lichtenstein, beckoning to him not to quit the Duke's side, placed himself boldly in front, and directing one more glance to his lord and son, closed his vizor, and cried, "Forwards! Here's to good Würtemberg for ever!"

About two hundred horsemen composed the resolute band, which moved on in a trot, arranged in the form of a wedge. The chancellor Ambrosius Bolland's heart beat lighter when they departed, for the Duke, amidst the anxieties of the moment, had quite lost sight of him, and he now held council with himself how he could most conveniently dismount from his long-legged steed. The noble beast, however, with upstanding ears and restless motion had noticed the departure of the cavalry. So long as they moved on in gentle trot, he remained tolerably quiet. But when the trumpets sounded the attack, and the gallant crew broke into a gallop with Würtemberg's banner waving high above the helmet plumes, this appeared to be the moment which the chancellor's high metaled steed had been anticipating, for with the rapidity of a bird, he stretched over the plain in the track of the other horsemen. His rider, almost deprived of his senses, and his hand seizing the pummel of his saddle in a state of convulsion, attempted to halloo, but the rapidity with which he cut through the air hindered all further utterance. Though the Duke and his friends had gained some considerable distance from him, the chancellor soon overtook, and then passing them, found himself, much against his will, the leading man in the desperate encounter which was about to take place. The attention of the enemy was riveted to the extraordinary figure of the chancellor, which appeared more like an ape in armour than a warrior on horseback, and before they could make out what he was, his steed had carried him into the midst of their ranks. The spectacle was so highly ridiculous, that the Würtembergers, notwithstanding this moment was for them one of life or death, broke out into loud laughter, which, spreading confusion among the troops of the League, composed of those of Ulm, Gmünd, Aulen, Nürnberg, and other imperial cities, allowed the overpowering weight of the two hundred horses, carrying the chancellor along with them, to break through, and gain the rear of their enemies. They pushed on their march in haste, and before the Leaguist cavalry could be sent in pursuit, the Duke, with his followers, had already gained a long start, and turned off the field of battle by a side path.

The mounted burghers having covered the retreat of the Duke, he effected his escape with a few faithful adherents, whilst they directed their route towards Stuttgardt. The enemy's cavalry only came up with them just as they had reached the gates of the city, when great was their disappointment not to capture either the Duke or any of his principal partisans, whom they expected to find among them. Ambrosius Bolland was their only prize. He, more dead than alive from excessive fright and fatigue, was not able to dismount from his elevated position without assistance. After having peeled his body of its unaccustomed covering, the Leaguists vented their rage and disappointment upon the unfortunate man, by beating him and other ill-usage; for they attributed to his supposed bravery, which appeared to them to exceed all they had ever witnessed, the loss of a thousand gold florins, set as a reward upon the capture of the Duke. And so it happened that the gallant chancellor, not like his master beaten in battle, was beaten after it.

CHAPTER XXXIV

Think on the many gallant deeds
One valiant hand has done,
And follow where your country needs,
Where a hero's grave is won.
Here, here they flee! pursue the way they go:
The light of heaven shows our flying foe.

L. Uhland.

The Duke and his followers passed the night after the day of the decisive battle in a narrow deep ravine of a wood, which, being surrounded by high rocks and thick underwood, offered a safe retreat for the moment, and is called, to this day, "Ulerich's cavern," by the people of the country. It was the fifer of Hardt who appeared again as a saviour in their flight, and led them to this place, known only to the peasantry and shepherds of the neighbourhood. The Duke determined to repose in this secluded spot, and, as soon as the following day broke, to continue his flight towards Switzerland. He would have preferred continuing his route under cover of the night, as being more favourable to elude the vigilance of his enemies. The fate of the disastrous day having given them full possession of the country again, it seemed next to impossible to escape through their numerous patroles, which would now scour the country to intercept his retreat. Delay was therefore dangerous; but the horses being unable to proceed after the heat and fatigue of the battle, he was compelled by necessity to run the risk of taking a short rest.

The party seated themselves around a small fire. Sleep soon came to the Duke's aid, and for awhile made him forget that he had again lost his dukedom. The knight of Lichtenstein also slept. Maxx Stumpf von Schweinsberg, resting his arms on his knees, concealed his face in both hands, and it was uncertain whether he dosed, or whether he was sorrowing over the fate of his unhappy master, which the day's battle had so cruelly decided. Albert von Sturmfeder, though almost overpowered with fatigue, resisted the power of sleep, and, being the youngest of the party, volunteered to keep watch. Beside him sat his faithful friend, the fifer of Hardt, his eyes fixed steadfastly on the fire, and appeared to concentrate his thoughts in the words of a song, whose melancholy strain he hummed to himself with a soft suppressed voice. When the fire blazed up occasionally a little brisker, he cast a sorrowful look at the Duke, to see if he still slept, and then recommenced the same lamentable dirge.

"You are singing a very melancholy strain, Hans!" said Albert, whose attention was excited by the peculiar tones of the song: "it sounds like a death song or mourning dirge; I can't listen to it without shuddering."

"Death may knock at every man's door at any moment," replied the fifer, looking still more gloomily at the fire; "I like to occupy my mind upon such subjects, for it often strikes me, I would prefer going out of this world with similar thoughts in my mind."

"But how is it you think more upon death at this moment than at other times, Hans? You were always a merry fellow at harvest time; and your guitar never failed being heard at a wake. You certainly never sang a death-song on such occasions."

"My happiness is gone," he answered, and pointed to the Duke; "all my anxieties and troubles have been in vain. His star is set, and I----I am his shadow; therefore nothing is left for me. If I had not a wife and child, I would willingly die this very night."

"You were, indeed, his faithful shadow," said the young man, moved at these words: "I have always admired your fidelity. Listen, Hans! it will perhaps be some time before we see each other again; and having now time and opportunity to converse together, tell me, if it be not too much to ask, what has bound you so close and exclusively to the fortunes of the Duke?"

The man was silent a few minutes, and trimmed the burning embers of the fire. A troubled look beamed in his eyes, leaving Albert in doubt whether he had not touched upon a subject which was painful to his friend, whose countenance he thought was tinged with a passing blush. "That question," he at length replied, "refers to a certain occurrence, which I never willingly speak about. But you are right, sir, in your conjecture, and it appears to me also that we shall not meet again for some time; therefore I will satisfy your curiosity. Have you ever heard of the insurrection called, 'Poor Conrad'?"

"O, yes!" replied Albert, "the report spread far beyond Franconia. Was it not an insurrection of the peasantry? It was said, they wanted even to take the Duke's life!" I----

"You are perfectly right, the affair of Conrad was a bad thing. About seven years ago many men among us peasantry were dissatisfied with our landlords; great distress prevailed throughout the country, in consequence of the failure of the crops. The rich had squandered all their money; the poor had long since no more left, but still we were obliged to pay heavy taxes without end, in order to satisfy the exorbitant demands of the Duke's court, where every luxury was carried on in the midst of an impoverished country."

"Did your representatives accede to these extravagant demands?" inquired the young man.

"They did not always venture to say no; for, the Duke's purse having an enormous large hole in it, they had no other means of repairing it than by the sweat of our brow. Many, therefore, struck work, because, said they, 'the corn which we sow, does not grow for our bread, and the wine we make, does not flow into our casks.' They then thought, as nothing more could be taken from them than their lives, that they would live merrily and without care, and calling themselves counts of 'no home,' spoke of their many castles on the 'hungry mountain,' of their wealthy possessions in 'the land of famine' and on the banks of the 'river of beggary.' This was the origin of the insurrection named 'The League of Poor Conrad.'"

The fifer of Hardt laid his head in his hand in deep thought, and was silent.

"But you promised to relate to me your adventures with the Duke," said Albert.

"I had nearly forgotten that," he answered: "well," he continued, "persecution was at length brought to such a pass, that even the weights and measures were decreased in size and quantity, so that the Duke and his courtiers might be the gainers at our expense. We paid the same for a less quantity. The consequence of this species of tyranny gave rise to a circumstance which, commencing at first in mere joke, became a source of bitter hatred and revenge. Many could not bear the thought of this act of flagrant injustice, by which every one else had full weight and measure, whilst we alone, the peasantry, were the sufferers. Poor Conrad carried the weights into the valley of the Rems, and made a proof by water."

"A proof by water,--what's that?" asked the young man.

"Ha!" laughed Hans, "that is an easy way of proving a thing. A stone of a pound weight was paraded to the sound of drum and fife to the banks of the Kerns, and they said, 'if it swims, the Duke is right; if it sinks, the peasant is right.' The stone sank, and Poor Conrad armed himself. All the peasants then rose in the vallies of the Rems and Neckar, and throughout all the country up to Tübingen far over the Alb, and demanded the old laws.

The members of the diet were assembled and harangued them, but all to no purpose, they would not disperse."

"But you--what part did you take? You; don't say a word about yourself," said Albert.

"That's said in a very few words," replied Hans: "I was one of the most violent among them. Never being much inclined to work, and having been inhumanly punished for transgressing the game laws, I joined Poor Conrad, and soon became as desperate as Gaispeter and Bregenzer. The Duke, seeing that the insurrection was becoming dangerous, came himself to Schorndorf. We had been called to that place for the purpose of swearing allegiance. Many hundreds appeared, but all armed. Ulerich addressed us himself; but we would not hear him. The marshal of the empire then stood up, and raising his gold staff said, 'He who holds to Duke Ulerich von Würtemberg, let him come over to his side!' Gaispeter also stepping upon a large stone, cried, 'He who holds to Poor Conrad of Hungry Hill, come over here!' The Duke stood alone among his servants, deserted by his people: we, the opposite party, remained with the beggar."

"Oh, what a shameful transaction," cried Albert, moved by a feeling of the injustice which caused it, "but more particularly so in those who allowed it to go to such lengths! I'll be bound Ambrosius Bolland, the chancellor, was mostly to blame in it."

"You are not far wrong," replied the fifer; "but hear me. When the Duke saw that all was lost, he threw himself on his horse. We crowded about him, but no one was bold enough to touch his person, for we were staggered by his commanding look. 'What is it you want, you scum of the earth?' he cried, and giving his horse the spur, made him bound in the air, by which three men were knocked down. This awakened our fury; the people laid hold of the horse's reins, they thrusted at him with their spears, and I so far forgot myself as to seize him by the mantle, crying, 'Shoot the villain dead!'"

"Was that you, Hans?" cried Albert, and eyed him with a look of horror.

"That was I," he uttered slowly and in a subdued tone, evidently suffering from the recollection of the deed. "But the Duke escaped from us, and assembled a force which we were not able to contend with, and we surrendered unconditionally. Twelve leaders of the insurrection were conducted to Schorndorf, tried and condemned; I was one of them. When I was in prison, with leisure to think of the wrong I had done, and contemplate the approach of death, I shuddered at myself, and was ashamed of being associated with such miserable fellows as the other eleven were."

"But how were you saved?" asked Albert.

"In the way I have already related to you in Ulm; by a miracle. We twelve were conducted to the market-place, for the purpose of being beheaded. The Duke was seated in front of the town-hall, and ordered us to be brought before him again. My eleven companions threw themselves on their knees, causing the noise of their chains to resound through the air, crying for mercy in pitiable tones. He fixed his eyes upon them for some time, and then, observing that I alone remained silent, said, 'Why do not you beg for pardon also?' 'My Lord,' I answered, 'I know what I deserve: may God hare mercy on my soul!' Without saying a word, he looked at us some time longer, and then made a sign to the executioner. We were brought up to the scaffold according to our ages; and I being the youngest, was the last. I remember little more of that terrible moment; but I shall never forget the frightful sound of the axe when it severed the heads from the bodies of the culprits."

"For God's sake, say no more on the subject!" Albert requested; "but pass on to the rest of the story."

"Nine heads were stuck upon the points of spears, when the Duke cried, 'Ten shall bleed, but two shall be pardoned. Let dice be brought: he who throws the lowest number in three throws, loses his head.' The dice-box was given to me first, but I said, 'I have forfeited my life, and I will not gamble for it.' The Duke said, 'Well; I'll throw for you.' The box was then handed to the other two. They shook the dice with cold trembling hand, and threw. One counted nine, and the other fourteen; the Duke then seized the box, and shook it. He looked at me hard in the face, but I did not tremble. He threw, and covered the dice with his hand. 'Beg for mercy,' said he, 'there is still time.' 'I pray you to pardon the rash act,' I answered, 'but I beg not for mercy, because I don't deserve it.' He raised his hand; and behold, he counted eighteen! The effect it produced on me was indescribable; I thought the Duke sat in God's stead in judgment. I fell upon my knees, and vowed to live and die in his service. The tenth man was beheaded, and two of us saved."

Albert had listened to the tale of the fifer of Hardt with increasing interest, and when he finished it, and noticed his bold expressive eyes filled with tears, he could not resist taking him by the hand, saying, "Truly, you have been guilty of a heavy crime against the Lord of your country, but you have also expiated it dearly by being brought so near to death. The terror of immediate death, whilst the sword of vengeance is hanging over a guilty head, must indeed be tenfold more appalling when the culprit is obliged to witness the execution of so many acquaintances, awaiting the slow approach of his own last moment along with them; but you have faithfully atoned to your prince for laying your hand upon his person, by a life of fidelity, sacrifices, and risks of all kinds in his cause. And how often have you liberated him from danger, perhaps saved his life! Truly you have richly redeemed your debt."

The poor man, when he had finished his story, relapsed into gloomy thought, with his eyes fixed on the fire; and had it not been, that an occasional sad smile passed over his countenance when Albert spoke to him, he had all the appearance of being totally unconscious of what was going on around him. "Do you mean," said he, "that I could ever sufficiently repent, and redeem the crime of which I have been guilty? No; such debts are not so easily liquidated, and a redeemed life must be devoted to the service of him who has saved it. To wander among mountains, getting intelligence from an enemy's camp, and finding out places of concealment, are but trifling services, sir, and cannot satisfy the mind under such circumstances. I feel convinced that I must die for him one of these days; and then I pray you take care of my wife and child."

A tear fell on his beard; but, as if ashamed of his weakness, he hastily wiped it away, and continued: "Could but the sacrifice of my life ward off the impending danger which surrounds him--could my death erase that unfortunate oath of allegiance, which he has imposed on the country, and replace him in the hearts of his people; I would willingly die in that hour!"

The Duke awoke. He raised himself up, and surveyed the surrounding rocks and trees, with his companions seated around the faint glimmering of burning embers, with astonishment, as if he had been transported by magic to this wild spot. Covering his face with his hands, and then gazing about him again, to convince himself whether the appearance of these objects were reality or not, he first glanced at one and then at another with painful feelings. "I have this day lost my country again," said he, "but that event has not given me so much trouble as I feel at this moment, for I dreamt I re-possessed it, and saw it in higher bloom than ever. Alas, it was but a dream!"

"You must not be ungrateful, sir," said Maxx Stumpf von Schweinsberg, raising himself from his bent position: "be not unthankful for nature's kindness. Think how much more miserable you would have been, if in sleep, which should give you renewed strength to bear the burden of your misfortunes, you had still felt the weight of them. When you laid down to rest, you were overcome by the fatal result of the day, but now your features assume a kindlier and milder appearance; have we not, then, cause to be thankful for your soothing dream?"

"I would I had never seen the day again!" replied Ulerich. "Oh, that I could have been lost in the pleasures of that same dream for centuries, and then have come to life again,--it was so beautiful, so consoling!"

He laid his head on his hand, and appeared oppressed with grief. The conversation roused the knight of Lichtenstein. He was acquainted with the character of Ulerich, and knew the necessity of not allowing him to give way to his feelings, and, particularly at this critical moment, not to let him brood over the terrible loss he had sustained; he therefore drew nearer to him, and said:

"Well, sir, perhaps you will tell us what you dreamt of? It may, perchance, afford your friends some consolation also; for you must know, I have faith in dreams, especially when they occupy our minds in hours of importance, and are fraught with destiny; I believe they are sent from above to raise our hopes, and arm us with fortitude."

The Duke remained silent some time longer, apparently pondering over the last words of his old friend. He then began, "My brother-in-law, William of Bavaria, has burnt the castle of my ancestors this day, as a proof of his friendship. The Würtembergers have been established there from time immemorial, and the country which we possess takes its name from the same castle. He seems to have fired it with the torch of death, and with its flames to have wished to exterminate the arms, the remembrance, nay, even the very name of Würtemberg, from the face of the earth. He has partially succeeded; for my only son, young Christoph, is in a distant land; my brother, George, has no child; and I--I have been beaten and driven out; they have repossessed my country, and where can I look to the hope of returning to it again?"

Ulerich was again silent. His mind appeared occupied with a subject too great for utterance. A peaceful serenity lay on the features of the unfortunate Prince, and an unusual expression beamed in his eyes as he directed them upwards to heaven. His companions looked at him in awful expectation of hearing some important communication resulting from his dream.

"Listen further," he continued: "I gazed on the charming valley of the Neckar. The river flowed on in its accustomed gentle winding blue stream. The valley and hills appeared lovely, and more luxuriant than ever. The woods on the heights and the meadows assumed the aspect of one continued garden, spreading their rich green vineyards from hill to hill, and in the valley below full-bearing fruit trees without number completed the blooming scene. I stood enchanted and riveted to the view; the sun shone with greater splendour than usual, the blue vault of heaven was lighted up more brilliantly than I had ever witnessed it, and all nature seemed dressed in brighter colours than mortal eye had ever beheld. When I raised my intoxicated eye, and gazed upon the valley of the Neckar, I beheld a castle pleasantly situated on the summit of a hill which rose from the banks of the river, with the rays of the morning sun playing upon its walls. The sight of this peaceful habitation rejoiced my heart, for there were no ditches or high defences, no towers or battlements, no portcullis nor drawbridge, to remind the beholder of the contentions of men, and of the uncertain history of mortals.

"And as I was wrapped in astonishment and delight in the contemplation of the peaceful aspect of the valley and the unguarded castle, I turned round, and beheld the walls of my castle no longer to exist. Here, at least, my dream did not deceive me, for yesterday I saw the battlements fall, and the watch-tower sink, over which my banner had formerly floated. No stone of Würtemberg was more to be seen, but in its place stood a temple, ornamented with pillars and cupola, such as is to be found in Rome and Greece. Meditating how all this change could have come to pass, I observed some men in foreign costume, not far from me, inspecting the country.

"One of these men, in particular, drew my attention. He led a beautiful youth by the hand, and pointed out to him the valley which lay at their feet, the surrounding mountains, the river, the towns and villages in the neighbourhood, and in the distance. Upon a closer inspection, I observed the man had the features of my brother George, and it struck me that he must belong to the race of my ancestors, and be a true Würtemberger. He descended with the boy from the hill into the valley below, followed by the other man at a respectful distance. I stopped the last man, and asked him who the other person was that had described the country to the lad; 'That was the King,' said he, and followed the rest."

The Duke was silent, and looked inquisitively at the knights, as if to hear their opinion. No one answered for some time, at length the knight of Lichtenstein said, "I am now sixty-five years old, and have seen and heard much in the world; many things come to pass which astonish the human mind, but in which a pious man may distinguish the finger of God. Believe me, that dreams also are of his sending, as nothing happens upon earth without some reason. As there were seers and prophets in ancient times, why should not the Lord send one to his saints in our days, to open the dark gates of futurity to the mind of an unfortunate man through the channel of a dream, and give him an insight into coming happier days? Despond not, therefore, my lord! The enemy has burnt your castle--in one day you have lost a dukedom; but your name will nevertheless not become extinct, and your remembrance will not be washed out from Würtemberg's history."

"A King----" said the Duke, thoughtfully, "I dare not presume, now that I am an outcast, to think of a King springing from my race. Is it not possible that Satan may tempt us with such dreams, for the purpose of deceiving us afterwards more cruelly?"

"But why have doubts of futurity?" said Schweinsberg, smiling. "Could any one of your noble ancestors have thought their family would have become Dukes of the country, and their beautiful land have borne the name of Würtemberg? Let your dream console you, which has been given as a hint of the destiny awaiting your family. Believe that your name is destined to nourish in distant, very distant times, in the land of your forefathers, and that in remote ages the Princes of Würtemberg will bear the features of your generation."

"Well, then, I will hope so," replied Ulerich von Würtemberg; "I will continue to hope, that the country will still hold to us, dark as our present lot may appear. May our grand-children never experience such hard times as we have, and may it ever be said they are--fearless."

"And faithful!" added the fifer of Hardt, with emphasis, as he rose from his seat. "But it is high time, my Lord Duke, to set out. The dawn of morn is not far distant; we must pass the Neckar at all hazards before daylight."

They all rose, and buckled on their arms. The horses being brought forward, they mounted, and the fifer of Hardt went on before to lead the way out of the place of concealment. The escape of the Duke was attended with considerable danger, for the enemy sought all possible means to take him prisoner. To gain the road by which he might elude the vigilance of his enemies, it was absolutely necessary to repass the Neckar; and to accomplish this in safety was no easy matter. Heavy rains had swollen the river to such a degree, that it appeared next to impossible to pass it on horseback by swimming. The bridges, for the most part, were occupied by the troops of the League. But Hans had taken the precaution to ascertain by the aid of faithful friends, that the bridge of Köngen was still open, having been given to understand that the enemy had thought it needless to guard it, as, being so near Esslingen and their own camp, they never dreamt the Duke would venture to come that way. This path, therefore, Ulerich chose as the safest, though it still appeared attended with great danger, and the party set out towards the Neckar in deep silence, and with caution.

When they reached the fields beyond the wood, the dawn of morning tinged the horizon; and having gained a better road, they rode on at a brisk pace, and soon got a sight of the glimmering of the Neckar, not far from the high vaulted bridge which they were to pass. At this moment Albert, happening to look round, perceived a considerable number of horsemen coming towards them. He immediately made it known to his companions, who, counting above twenty-five horses, felt assured they could be no other than a party of cavalry of the League; the Duke's men having been dispersed, it was not likely any stragglers were in this neighbourhood.

These men, however, appeared not to remark the Duke's small retinue. To gain the bridge with the least possible delay, before they were hailed and questioned by this party, was of the utmost importance. The fifer of Hardt hastened on before, the Duke and his faithful knights followed in full trot, and as they increased their distance from the Leaguists, each felt lighter at heart, for they all were less anxious about their own lives than to secure the escape of Ulerich.

Having reached the bridge, and arrived on the middle of it, which was highly arched, twelve men sprang forward from behind the walls, armed with spears, swords, and guns, arresting the Duke's further progress. Perceiving he was discovered, he made a sign to his followers to retreat. Lichtenstein and Schweinsberg, being the two last, turned their horses, to retrace their steps, but to their dismay found themselves hemmed in by the cavalry they had first seen, who had galloped up in their rear, and at this instant occupied the entrance to the bridge.

It was still too dark to be able to distinguish the enemy with precision, who were, however, not backward in making themselves known. "Surrender yourself, Duke of Würtemberg," cried a voice, which appeared familiar to the knights; "you have no chance of escape."

"Who are you, to whom Würtemberg should surrender?" answered the Duke, with a furious voice, whilst he drew his sword; "you are no knight, for you don't sit on horseback."

"I am Doctor Calmus," replied the other, "and am ready to return the many kind acts I have received from you. I am a knight, for you yourself created me a donkey knight, and in return I will now dub you the knight without horse. Dismount, I say, in the name of the most illustrious League."

"Give me room, Hans," whispered the Duke, with a suppressed voice to the fifer, who stood between him and the doctor, with his axe raised to his shoulder in attitude of defence, "just stand on one side. Close in, my friends: we'll fall on them suddenly, and perhaps may succeed in cutting through." Albert was the only one who heard this order, for the other two knights were ten paces at least in their rear, already engaged with the Leaguist cavalry, who were unable to force their way past the gallant men to get at the Duke. Albert, therefore, closed with the Duke, with the intention of making a rush with him through the ranks of his opponents; but the doctor, perceiving it, called out to his people, "At him, my men! that's him in the green cloak; take him, dead or alive!" pushing forward at the same time to the attack. He carried a spear of unusual length, and made a thrust at Ulerich, which might have been fatal, for it was still dark, and the Duke did not remark it immediately; but the quick-sighted Hans parried the thrust of the renowned Doctor Calmus, which was on the point of piercing the breast of his master, and with one blow of his axe felled him to the ground, where he lay sprawling among his companions. They were staggered at the deadly blow of the countryman, who, wielding his axe high in the air, drove them back a few paces. Albert took advantage of this moment to possess himself of the Duke's cloak, which he threw over his own shoulders, and whispered to him to give his horse the spur, and force him over the breastwork of the bridge. Ulerich cast a look at the high swollen waters of the Neckar, and then up to heaven, in doubtful despair. Escape appeared hopeless. The fearful leap was his only choice between life or death, or falling into the hands of his enemies. A circumstance, however, arrested his attention for a moment before he decided upon it.

The enemy, with outstretched spears, advanced on the Duke. The fifer still kept his ground, though wounded and bleeding in many places, beating them down with his axe. His eyes flashed fire, his bold features carried the expression of joyful animation, and the smile about his mouth did not indicate despair; no, his noble soul feared not the approach of death, he rather looked to it in proud anticipation, as the reward for all the troubles and dangers he had taken upon himself. As he cut one of his opponents to the ground with his right hand, the halberd of another pierced his breast, that true breast, which even in death proved a faithful shield to his unhappy prince, for whom a more gallant heart never beat: he staggered, and sank to the ground. Casting his dying eye upon his master, "My lord Duke, we are quits," were his last words, which he uttered with a smile upon his countenance, and fell lifeless at his feet.

The Leaguists passing over his body, pressed hard upon the Duke, with the cry of exultation when Albert threw himself in the midst, his sword dealing destruction among his enemies. He was the last and only remaining defence of Duke Ulerich of Würtemberg; had he been overpowered, imprisonment or death to his friend and benefactor were unavoidable. The Duke, therefore, turned to the only means of escape; a desperate one indeed. He cast a painful look at the corpse of that man who had sealed his fidelity with his death, and turning his powerful war-horse on one side, gave him the spur that made him spring in the air, and with one desperate leap he cleared the breastwork of the bridge, carrying his princely rider down into the waters of the Neckar.

Albert ceased to defend himself. His eye was fixed solely on the Duke. The horse and rider plunged deep into the river; but the powerful beast, combating the eddies and current, soon appeared on its surface, carrying his master down the stream with the apparent ease and safety of a boat. All this was the affair of a few moments. Some of the Leaguists were for following him along the banks of the river, to seize the bold knight when he landed; but one of them nearest Albert cried, "Let him swim, he is not the right one; here is the prize, in the green cloak,--seize him." Albert, looking up to heaven in grateful thanksgiving for the escape of the Duke, and dropping his sword, surrendered to the Leaguists. They surrounded him, and willingly allowed him to dismount, to pay the last painful offices to the corpse of that man who had been their fearful opponent. Albert took his hand, with which he still kept a firm grasp of his blood-stained axe; it was icy cold. He felt his heart, to discover if there was still life in it; the deadly thrust of the spear had but too faithfully done its office. That eye once so bold was now lifeless, that mouth which bespoke an unbending cheerful mind was closed, the features rigid; but still the smile, that last dying salute with which he greeted his master, played upon his lips. Albert's tears fell on his faithful friend, as he pressed for the last time the cold hand of the fifer of Hardt; he closed his eyes, and, throwing himself upon his horse, followed his enemies to their camp.

CHAPTER XXXV

Happy the soldier, all his perils o'er,

In peace returning to his native place,

When those who love him meet him at the door,

And gaze with rapture on the wish'd-for face.

Schiller.

After a march of three hours, the troop of the Leaguists' soldiers, with their prisoner in the midst, approached their camp. Though they did not venture to talk aloud, it was easy to perceive, by their countenances, how great was their exultation at their supposed triumph and prize, and it did not escape the acute observation of Albert that the whisper among them referred to the reward they were likely to gain for the person of the Duke. A feeling of satisfaction filled the breast of the young man, in the hope that his unhappy Prince might gain time to escape his enemies by the diversion the bold sacrifice he had made of himself in his favour. But the thought which now gave him the greatest uneasiness was the distress his beloved wife would experience, when she became acquainted with the result of the battle. Though he had informed her, through the medium of faithful messengers, of his having escaped unhurt in the bloody conflict, she was still ignorant of the unfortunate turn in the Duke's fate; still less could she know his own. He could well imagine her state of mind, when, among the prisoners brought into Stuttgardt, neither her father nor husband were found of the number. The thought was agonising to his mind, rendered doubly so amidst the taunts of those who now led him as a prisoner to the presence of his enemies. These, and a thousand other painful feelings, chilled his joy in having been the saviour of his friend.

Could he hope to be liberated a second time by the League, as he had been in Ulm? Taken with arms in his hand,--known as the most zealous friend of the Duke,--his only prospect was a long imprisonment, and harsh treatment. The arrival at the advanced posts of the camp interrupted these gloomy thoughts. One of the troop which guarded him was sent on before to acquaint the commanders of the League of their prisoner, and to receive their orders respecting the place where he was to be brought. This was a painful quarter of an hour for Albert. He wished of all things, if possible, to speak to Fronsberg, hoping that this noble friend of his father might still retain a kindly feeling towards him, and, at least, judge him more favourably than Truchses von Waldburg and many others, who he well knew to be inimical towards him.

The man returned with orders to conduct the prisoner as quietly as possible, and without ceremony, to the large tent in which the officers generally held their council of war. For this purpose they turned off by a side path, and the soldiers begged Albert to close the vizor of his helmet, that he might pass unknown, till he arrived before the council. He willingly complied with this request, for nothing was more painful to his feelings than to be exposed to the gaze of the curious or exulting multitude. Numerous serving men were assembled here, whose different costumes and badges of distinction led Albert to suppose a large assemblage of nobles and knights were congregated in the tent.

The news that a troop of infantry had taken a man of distinction prisoner, appeared to have preceded his arrival, for when Albert threw himself from his saddle, the people crowded around him, and, with looks of curiosity, tried to get a sight of his features through the apertures of his vizor. A page of honour with difficulty made his way through the multitude, having been sent, "in the name of the commanders of the League," to open a road by which the prisoner could reach the tent. Three of the men who had taken him were ordered to follow; their joy was unbounded, and they thought of nothing less than receiving immediately the gold florins which had been offered as the price for the person of the Duke of Würtemberg.

The inner curtain of the tent being drawn up, Albert walked in boldly and with a firm, step, looking round upon the men who were to decide upon his fate. Many known faces were among the number, who eyed him with inquisitive penetrating looks. The scowling glance and inimical front of Truchses von Waldburg were still fresh in his memory, and the scornful exulting expression of the features of this man did not augur him any good. Sickingen, Alban von Closen, Hutten, all sat before him as at that time when he bid the League an eternal farewell. But when he beheld that noble figure, those dignified features of Fronsberg, which were deeply engraven on his grateful heart, he felt self convicted in his own estimation. It was not contempt or triumphant joy which sat upon his features,--no, it was an expression of sorrowing thoughtfulness, with which an honourable man receives a valiant conquered enemy.

Albert now stood before these men, when Truchses von Waldburg began:--"The Swabian League has at last the honour of seeing the illustrious

Duke of Würtemberg before them. The invitation which you sent to us was certainly much too courteous, but----"

"You are mistaken," answered Albert, raising the vizor of his helmet at the same time. The members of the League started when they beheld the fine countenance of the young knight, as if they had seen Minerva's shield and Medusa's head.

"Ha! traitors! base villains! dogs!" cried Truchses to the three soldiers; "what cub do you bring here in the place of the Duke? The very sight of him excites my bile! Tell me quickly what has become of him--speak!"

The soldiers turned pale. "Is he not the right one?" they asked. "That was him with the green cloak."

Truchses trembled with rage, his eyes darted fire, he would have executed the soldiers upon the spot, and talked of hanging them; but the rest of the knights compelled him to curb his violence; and Hutten, pale with anger also, but more composed than the other, asked, "Where is Doctor Calmus? let him come forward, to give an account of himself, for he volunteered to arrest the Duke."

"Ah, sir!" replied one of the soldiers, "his account is already settled; he lies dead on the bridge of Köngen."

"Killed?" cried Sickingen, "and the Duke fled! relate the circumstance, villains!"

We placed ourselves in ambush near the bridge, as the doctor ordered us. It was still dark, when we heard the tread of horses approach the bridge, and at the same time perceived the signal which our cavalry on the other side of it had agreed to make as soon as the Duke's party issued from the wood. "Now is the time," cried the doctor; "we instantly got up and occupied the exit from the bridge. As far as we could distinguish, four horsemen and a peasant formed the party. The two hindermost turned back and engaged our cavalry, whilst the other two, and the peasant, attacked us.

"We stretched out our lances, the doctor calling to them to surrender; but they paid no attention to the summons, and fell on us with determined fury. The man in the green mantle was pointed out as the prize, and we should soon have had him had it not been for the peasant,--if it was not, indeed, the very devil himself,--who with his axe felled the doctor and two of our comrades in a trice. One of our party revenged our leader's life by running the peasant through the body with his halbert, which encouraged us to renew our attack on the man in the green mantle. His companion sprang his horse over the bridge into the Neckar, and swam down the river.

Having subdued the man who was our principal object, we let the other go, and brought the prisoner with us."

"That was Ulerich, and no other," cried Alban von Klosen. "Ha! to jump over the bridge into the river! no other man in the whole world would have dared to do so."

"We must follow him," Truchses exclaimed; "the whole of the cavalry must start immediately and hunt the banks of the river,--I myself will go----"

"Oh! sir," replied one of the soldiers, "you are too late; we left the bridge three hours ago, so that he will have got a long start, and, as no one knows the country better than he does, there is no chance of finding him."

"Fellow! do you mean to prescribe to me what to do?" cried Truchses in fury: "You allowed him to escape, and you shall be answerable for it. Call the guard--I'll have you hung at once!"

"Pray be just," said Fronsberg. "It was not the poor fellows' fault; they would have been too happy to have earned the money which was set on the Duke's head. The doctor was the cause of his escape, and you have already heard he is not alive to answer for it."

"It was you, therefore, who represented the person of the Duke," said Truchses, turning to Albert, who had calmly looked on during this scene. "You are always coming in my way, with your milk face. The devil employs you everywhere, when you are least wanted. This is not the first time that you have crossed my plans."

"No," replied Albert, "for when you fell upon the Duke, as you supposed, at Neuffen, it was I who crossed your path there also; and it was I whom your men cut down that night."

The knights were astonished to hear this, and looked inquisitively at Truchses. He reddened, but whether from anger or shame it was not known, and said, "What are you chattering about Neuffen? I know nothing about that affair. I only regret that when they cut you down you had ever risen again to appear before me this day a second time. But as it is, I rejoice to have you in my clutches. You have proved yourself the bitterest enemy of the League; you have acted in the service of the exiled Duke both openly and secretly, thereby sharing his offence against us and the whole empire. Beside these crimes, you have been taken this day with arms in your hands. You are therefore guilty of high treason against the most illustrious League of Swabia and Franconia."

"Your charges are highly ridiculous," replied the young man, in a tone of defiance: "you made me swear to remain neuter between the two parties for fourteen days, to which I faithfully adhered, so true as God is my witness. You have no right to require an account of my conduct since that time, for I was no longer bound to you: and as to what you say of my being taken with arms in my hand, I would ask you, noble knights, who among you would not defend his life to the last when he was attacked by six or eight men? I demand then, as my right, the treatment becoming the rank of knighthood; and therefore I am ready to swear to a six weeks' neutrality. You cannot require more of me."

"Would you prescribe laws to us?" said Truchses. "You have learned a good lesson, indeed, from the Duke. I think I hear him speaking; but not one step shall you take to your friends before you own where that old fox, your father-in-law, is, and the road the Duke has taken."

"The knight of Lichtenstein was taken prisoner by your cavalry," he replied; "but the road which the Duke has taken, I know not; and I am ready to give my word of honour upon it."

"To be treated as a knight, indeed!" said Truchses, with a sarcastic laugh; "there you deceive yourself altogether. You must first prove where you won the golden spur! No; such criminals as you, are, according to our laws, thrown into the lowest dungeons; and so I will commence with you."

"I think that unnecessary," interrupted Fronsberg. "I will answer for Albert von Sturmfeder that he has a right to the golden spurs; besides which, he saved the life of a noble belonging to the League. You cannot forget the evidence of Dieterich von Kraft, how, through the intercession of this knight, he was saved from an ignominious death, and was even set at liberty. He has a right, therefore, to the same treatment by us."

"I know you have always spoken a word for him, your darling child," rejoined Truchses; "but this once it is of no avail. He must be sent to the tower of Esslingen this very moment."

"I will stand bail for him," said Fronsberg. "I possess the right of a voice in council with the rest. Let it pass to the vote what is to be done with the prisoner. In the mean while, let him be conducted to my tent."

Albert cast a look of heartfelt gratitude at his kind noble friend, for having a second time saved him from a threatened danger. Truchses muttered an order to the guards to follow the orders of Fronsberg, who led their prisoner through the narrow paths of the camp to the tent of the commander of the infantry.

Shortly after he had arrived at his destination, the man to whom he was so highly indebted stood before him, but Albert could not find words to express his sense of gratitude and respect. Fronsberg smiled at his embarrassment, and embraced him. "No thanks, no excuses," said he. "Did I not already anticipate all this when we took leave of each other in Ulm? But you would not believe me, and were determined to bury yourself among the ruins of the castle of your ancestors. I do not blame you; for believe me the campaigns and storms of many wars have not yet hardened my heart so much as to make me forget the power of love."

"My friend, my father!" exclaimed Albert, blushing with joy.

"Yes, I am truly your father,--the friend of your father. I have often thought of you with pride, even when you stood opposed to me in the enemy's ranks. Your name, young as you are, will always be mentioned with respect; for fidelity and courage in an enemy are always highly esteemed by a man of honour. Most of us rejoice that the Duke has escaped, for what could we have done with him? Truchses might perhaps have committed a rash step, which we all might have had cause to repent."

"And what is my fate to be?" asked Albert. "Am I to remain long in prison? Where is the knight of Lichtenstein? Oh, my poor wife! may I not see her?"

Fronsberg smiled mysteriously. "That will be difficult to manage," said he. "You will be sent to a fortress under safe escort, and given over to a guard, who will have orders to watch you strictly, and from whose charge you will not escape so easily. But, be of good cheer; the knight of Lichtenstein will accompany you, and both of you must swear to a year's neutrality and imprisonment."

Fronsberg was now interrupted by three men, who stormed his tent;--it was Breitenstein and Dieterich von Kraft, leading the knight of Lichtenstein between them.

"Do I see you again, my brave lad?" cried Breitenstein, as he took Albert's hand. "You have played me a pretty trick; your old uncle made me promise, upon my soul, to make something out of you, which would do honour to the League, but you deserted to the enemy, cutting and slashing at us, and nearly gained the victory yesterday by your hot-brained, desperate attack on our artillery!"

"Every one to his taste," replied Fronsberg; "he did honour to his friends, even in the enemy's ranks."

The knight of Lichtenstein embraced his son. "He is in safety," he whispered to him. Their eyes beamed with joy, in having both been instrumental in saving their unhappy Prince. The old knight discovered the green mantle which still hung on the shoulders of his son, and said, in astonishment, a tear of joy starting to his eye, "Ah, now I understand how everything has come to pass; they mistook you for the Duke. What would have become of him but for your courage and presence of mind in the critical moment? Your bravery and foresight have achieved more than any of us, and, though we are prisoners, we are still conquerors! Come to my heart, thou most noble son!"

"And Maxx von Stumpf Schweinsberg!" asked Albert, "what has become of him? is he a prisoner also?"

"He cut his way through the enemy,--for who could withstand his arm? My old bones are powerless, I am of no more use; but he has joined the Duke, and will be of more assistance to him than fifty horsemen. But I did not see the fifer,--tell me, how did he come out of the fray?"

"As a hero," replied Albert, agitated by a feeling of deep regret at the recollection of him; "he was run through the body by a lance, and his corpse lies on the bridge."

"Dead!" cried Lichtenstein, and his voice trembled. "His was indeed a faithful soul,--may it rest in peace! His actions were noble, and he died true to his master, as all should do."

Fronsberg now approached them, and interrupted their conversation. "You appear much cast down," said he; "but be of good cheer and consolation, noble sir! the fortune of war is changeable, and your Duke will, in all probability, once more return to his native country. Who knows if it is not better that we should send him to foreign parts again for a short time? Put by your helmet and armour; your fight at breakfast time will not have spoiled your appetite for mid-day's meal. Seat yourself beside us. About noon I expect the guardian, who is to have charge of you in your confinement; until then, let's be cheerful."

"That's a proposition we can readily satisfy," cried Breitenstein. "Dinner is ready, gentlemen: you and I have not dined together, Albert, since that day in the townhall of Ulm. Come, and we'll make up for lost time."

Hans von Breitenstein seated himself with Albert next to him; the others followed his example; the servants brought the dinner, and wine made the knight of Lichtenstein and his son forget, for a time, their unfortunate situation of being in the enemy's camp, and the uncertainty of their fate, which, according to Fronsberg's assurance, was to be an imprisonment of long duration. Towards the end of the repast Fronsberg was called away, but he soon returned, and said, with a serious countenance, "Willingly as I would wish to enjoy your society some time longer, my friends, I am sorry to compel you to break up. The guard is without into whose charge I must deliver you, and I would advise you to lose no time, if you would arrive at the fortress of your confinement before dark."

"I trust our guard is one of our own rank,--a knight?" asked Lichtenstein, whilst his face assumed a gloomy, indignant frown. "I hope proper attention will be paid to our rights, and that we shall have an escort fitting our station."

"No knight will accompany you," said Fronsberg, "but a fitting escort, of which you shall convince yourself." With these words he raised the curtain of his tent, discovering to the astonished father and son the lovely features of Bertha. She flew into the arms of her enraptured husband. Her venerable father, speechless from joy and surprise, kissed his child on her forehead, and pressed the hand of the honest Fronsberg in token of heartfelt gratitude.

"That is your guardian," said the latter; "and the castle of Lichtenstein the place of your confinement. I can see already, in your eyes," addressing himself to Bertha, "that you will not be too severe with the young man, and that the old man will not have to complain. But let me advise you, my pretty daughter, to have a watchful eye to your prisoners; don't let them out of the castle, for fear of their rejoining the cause of certain people. Your pretty head will answer for their actions!"

"But, dear sir," replied Bertha, whilst she drew her beloved closer to her, and smiled playfully at the stern commander, "recollect he is my head,--so how can I command him?"

"That is just the reason why you should take care not to lose it again. Bind him fast with the knot of love,--let him not escape, for he easily changes his colours; of which we have had proofs sufficient."

"I only wore one colour, my fatherly friend!" replied the young man, looking at his beautiful wife, and pointing to the scarf which he wore, "only one, and to this I remained faithful."

"Well, then! remain true to it for the future," said Fronsberg, and gave him his hand to depart. "Farewell! your horses are before the tent: may you arrive happily at your destination, and think sometimes, in friendship, of old Fronsberg."

Bertha took leave of this worthy man with tears of grateful thanks in her eyes; the men also were overcome when they took his hand, for they were well aware that, without his kind interference, their fate might have been of a very different stamp. George von Fronsberg followed the happy party with his eye until they turned the corner of the long lane of tents. "He is in good hands," said he, as he turned to Breitenstein. "Truly the blessing of his father rests upon him. Not a better or more beautiful wife, and more honourable son, will be found in all Swabia."

"Yes, yes!" replied Hans von Breitenstein, "but he has not to thank his own wits or foresight for it. He who seeks to better his fortune, let him conduct a wife home. I am fifty years old, and still on the look-out for a partner; and you, also, Dieterich von Kraft, are you not upon the same scent?"

"Not at all,--quite the contrary,--I am already provided," he replied, as if awoke out of a dream; "when one sees such a couple, we know what is next to be done. I am going to put myself, this very hour, into my sedan, on my journey to Ulm, there to conduct my cousin Marie to my home. Farewell, my friends!"

When the Swabian League had reconquered Würtemberg, they re-established their government, and reigned over the whole country, as in the summer of 1519. The partisans of the exiled Duke were compelled to swear neutrality, and were banished to their respective castles. Albert von Sturmfeder and his family were included in this mild destiny, living retired on the Lichtenstein; and a new life of peaceable domestic happiness fell to the lot of the loving couple.

Often when they stood at the window of the castle, overlooking Würtemberg's beautiful fields, they would think of their unfortunate Prince, who also once viewed his country from the same spot. It reminded them of the chain of events of their own history, and of the extraordinary means by which their union had been brought about; and which they did not fail to acknowledge, would perhaps not have happened so soon, had their fate been otherwise ordained. But they felt the joy of their existence incomplete when they thought of the founder of their happiness, living in the misery of banishment far from his country.

Some years after the fatal battle, the Duke succeeded in re-conquering Würtemberg. The stern lesson of adversity and misfortune brought him back a wiser Prince and a happier man. He re-established the ancient rights and laws of the land, and won the hearts of his people by judicious measures. He enforced the preaching of holy doctrines, and by his example recommended the practice of them. The religious principles he had imbibed in foreign lands, and which had afforded him the only consolation amidst his sufferings, he now infused into the laws of his country, as the only sure foundation-stone of a people's happiness. Albert and his pious wife plainly discovered the finger of a merciful God watching over the fate of Ulerich von Würtemberg. They blessed Him who thus veils futurity from the eye of mortals, and, as in the present instance, turns dark into light to those who seek his guidance and protection in faith.

The name of Lichtenstein in Würtemberg became extinct at the death of the old knight; but he lived long enough to see his blooming grand-children attain the age of bearing arms. And in this way generation after generation pass over the face of the earth, new comers thrusting out old ones, and after a short lapse of fifty or an hundred years, the fame of honest men and faithful hearts is forgotten. The rushing stream of time drowns the voice of their remembrance, and only a few brilliant names float down the tide of history and play upon its surface in partial glittering light. Far more happy is the man whose actions carry their own silent worth along with them, finding their reward alone in the purity of conscience, and passing through life without courting the praise or flattery of the times in which he lived, nor living for the applause of after ages. The name of the fifer of Hardt and his actions, have come down to us in simple garb, through the medium of successive generations of shepherds in the neighbourhood of the "Misty Cavern." They relate the deeds of the man who concealed his unfortunate Duke among its deep recesses, as they conduct the stranger through their gloomy paths, and talk of the romantic events of Ulerich's life. The writer of history disdains such stories as unworthy of his pen; but they are not the less credible. When recounted on the spot, such as on the heights of Lichtenstein, where the Duke came every night at a stated hour to the castle, and when the place is pointed out on the bridge of Köngen, whence the undaunted man took the fearful leap into the deep waters below for life or death, we listen to the details with believing ears.

The old castle of Lichtenstein has long since fallen into ruin. A huntsman's house now occupies its foundations, light and airy, like a castle in the air, which imagination builds upon the ruins of antiquity. Würtemberg's fields spread themselves before the enchanted eye, rich and blooming as formerly, when Bertha by the side of her lover gazed upon them, and the most unhappy of her princes cast a farewell glance on his country from Lichtenstein's windows. The subterranean apartments of the castle, which received the exile, are still to be seen, in all their pride and glory; and the murmuring streams, gushing through the mysterious depths at the foot of the rock, would seem to relate events long since buried in oblivion.

It is a delightful custom of the inhabitants of the country, and also of the stranger from distant parts, to visit Lichtenstein and Ulerich's cavern on Whitsunday. Many hundreds of Swabia's children are attracted to these mountains on that day. They descend into the heart of the earth, whose crystal walls, lighted up by thousands of wax tapers, are made to reflect their sparkling beauties in numberless fantastic forms; they fill the cavern with the sound of the merry song, and listening to its echoes, which are accompanied by the melodious murmur of the running streams in the depth below, enjoy the wonders of nature's handy work. Having satisfied their curiosity, they return to the light of day, more pleased than ever with the glories of sunshine and the comfort of earth's blessings. Ascending the road leading to the heights of Lichtenstein, they arrive on its summit, where the men, surrounded by their wives and families, with the glass in the hand, overlook the distant fields, displayed to their view in all the lovely colours of the setting sun, and, with grateful hearts, thank heaven for the blessings of their father-land. The halls of Lichtenstein resound again with music, dancing, and the merry song, and the echo from its rocks seems to inspire the jovial guests with recollections of the former inmates of the castle, and with them to gaze upon good old Würtemberg. But whether the spirit of the lady of Lichtenstein, with that of Albert and the old knight, inspires them, or whether the faithful musician of Hardt quits his grave, and, as he was wont to do during his life, mounts up to the castle to cheer it with music and song, we know not. Often have we reposed on these rocks on a still summer's evening, enjoying the landscape, talking over the good old times, witnessing the sun's descent, and observing the castle, standing alone and solitary, lighted up by its last rays. Then it was we fancied we could distinguish, among the rustling of the trees, the sound of known voices, floating on the gentle breeze, wafting to our ears their salutations, and recounting the events of their past lives and actions. We have frequently experienced such like feelings, presenting to our imagination images, which fancy would realize before our eyes, and salute our ears with the whisper of their romantic tales, until at length we verily believed them to be,--the spirits of Lichtenstein.